SHUT UP & DRIVE

A Friends To Lovers Short Story

BAD BOYS MAKE GOOD DRIVERS
BOOK 1

GRACE NEWMAN

Box Box Publishing

Copyright © 2023 by Grace Newman

All rights reserved.

No part of this publication may be reproduced, distributed, or transmitted in any form or by any means, including photocopying, recording, or other electronic or mechanical methods, without the prior written permission of the publisher, except as permitted by U.S. copyright law. For permission requests, contact AuthorGraceNewman@Gmail.com.

The story, all names, characters, and incidents portrayed in this production are fictitious. No identification with actual persons (living or deceased), places, buildings, and products is intended or should be inferred.

Edited by Kellie G.

Copywriting by Jonathan N.

Artwork by Elena S.

❦ Created with Vellum

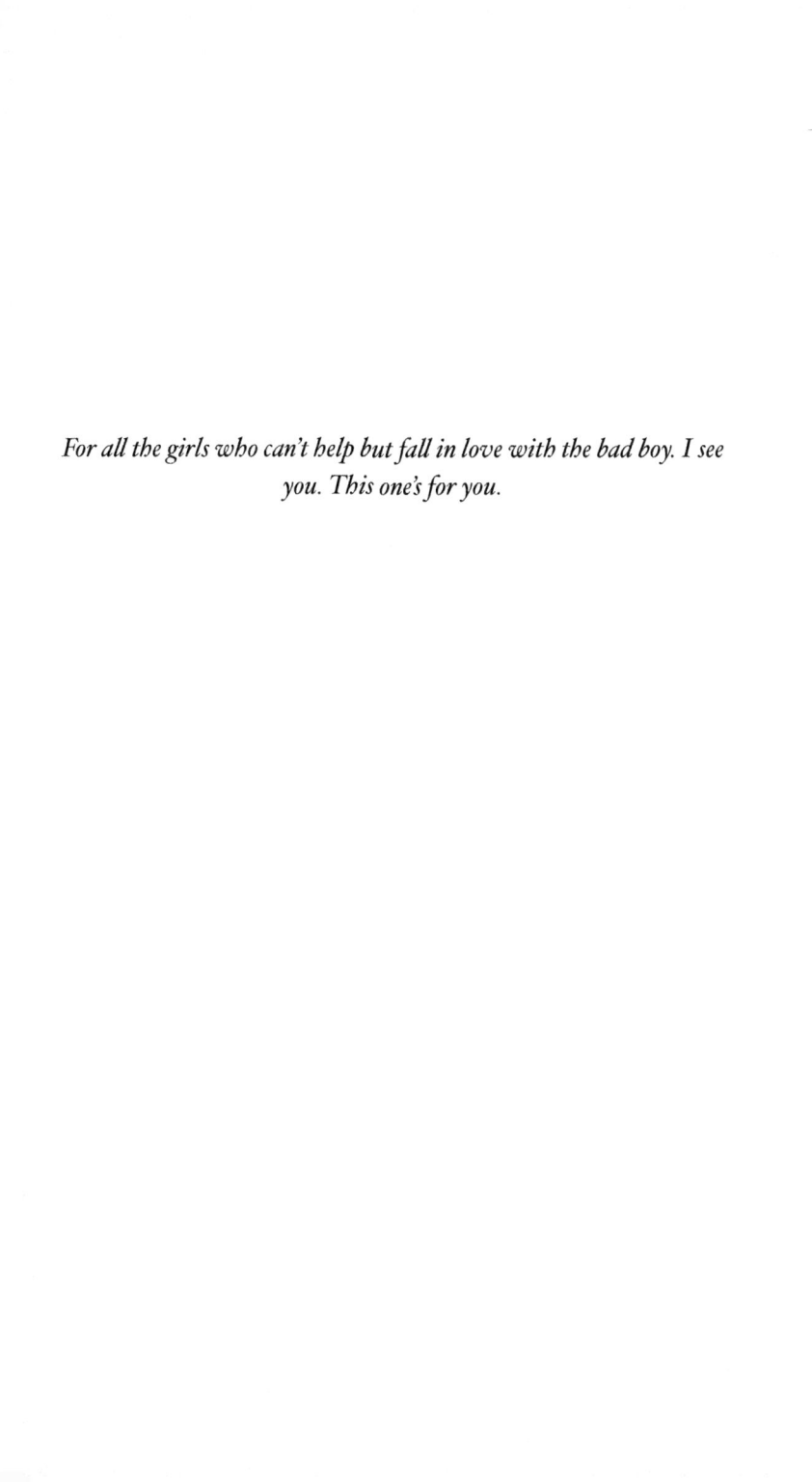

For all the girls who can't help but fall in love with the bad boy. I see you. This one's for you.

For every woman who has been ignored by a room full of men. ***Your time is coming.***

It's a widely known fact that all race car drivers are charismatic playboys ready to break your heart. Some hide it better than others, but under their suave exterior and charming good looks, there's a siren waiting to capture your heart and soul.

— POPPY

PROLOGUE

Poppy

2021 SEASON

"Okay, Ben. That's five laps to go."

"Roger." As I looked up from my computer screen, I glanced at the Sky Sports F1 coverage that was on the pit wall TVs.

You can do this Ben. This was our moment. If Ben won today, the championship would officially be ours.

"Back left is losing grip." I tried not to utter a frustrated sigh into my radio. Ben was incredibly *chatty* when he was nervous during a race. As his racing engineer, it was my job to be the epitome of calm and collected, even if all I wanted to do was tell him to *shut the fuck up and drive his goddamn car.*

"Four laps to go." Before I could revel in my curt radio message that I hoped had gotten my point across, I heard a barrage of yelling from the mechanics behind me.

Horror filled me first.

Then *dread*.

Then *fear*.

There on the television was the one thing I hated about this fucking sport – the crashes. As the Sky Sports camera panned away from the incident, I turned back to our cameras that had captured the incident, immediately replaying the footage. Liam had tried to make a daring corner move, a move that had forced his car into Ben's, which in return, sent them both spiraling off the track. The jolt of the impact caused Ben's car to flip in midair before tumbling down the ravine, crashing into the barriers at the bottom.

"Ben, can you hear me?" I frantically looked down at my computer to check for signs that his car was active.

"Ben?"

Radio silence.

A pang of guilt immediately hit me. Not one minute ago I was lambasting Ben's chattiness, and now all I wanted was to hear my best friend's voice.

I'd do anything to hear his voice on my damn radio.

Felix, our team principal, pulled me into the garage. A red flag had been issued, and the other cars were coming into the pits. There was still nothing on the television, but it was common practice in Formula 1 that television coverage never showed a dangerous accident until they had confirmation of the driver's wellbeing.

"Any news?"

"Marshalls have arrived on site. We should know in the next minute. Apparently, the car caught fire, and they had to put it out."

Over in the corner, I spotted Elise and Ben's mother, my Godmother, the two of them attempting to wave me over, but I just shook my head no, giving them a sympathetic look.

"... right, thank you. Appreciate it." Felix put his phone

back in his pocket, a smile creeping onto his face, and I felt relief immediately flood my body.

"He's alright. They have him in the safety car, he's lucid and walking." As soon as Felix said the words, the garage erupted into applause, and I knew that Sky Sports had just shown the coverage of Ben leaving his car.

"Let's head to the medical tent." I nodded at Felix and grabbed a few things, before rushing over to the makeshift medical office that was set up for races.

As soon as I walked in, I noticed Liam in the corner, getting his neck checked out by a physio. A nurse ushered me to another side of the building, and as soon as I saw Ben, I ran over, throwing my arms around him.

"Careful, Poppy," he chuckled. "Bit sore over here."

"Right, sorry... how are you feeling? You had us fucking scared over in the garage."

"I'll live." The corners of his mouth tipped up a tad, but I could see the weariness and exhaustion in his eyes – *and the disappointment.*

Four laps. That's how close we were to winning the championship.

"We'll get 'em next race, bud. Promise." Once Ben had received the all-clear from the doctor, we were immediately given instructions to head home.

"You know, why don't we take a left here? Get some extra air, hmm?" But before I could offer another convincing argument as to why we should take the long way round, Ben had spotted my reason for wanting to take a different route.

There, just a few meters ahead of us, was Liam Fitzgerald, the cause of this entire fiasco. I went to grab Ben's hand, but it was too late. He had already spotted Liam, and Ben was now barreling towards the Australian driver, his fists balled in anger at his sides.

"Hey, fuck face!"

"Jesus, Ben," I grumbled under my breath, cringing at his words. I ran after him, still attempting to get his attention, but he was too fast – *too angry* – to take notice. Liam turned around, and as soon as he saw Ben storming up to him, he, to his credit, took a step back.

"Can I *help* you?" Liam's tone told me he had zero interest in helping Ben with *anything* at that moment.

"You couldn't let me have it, could you? Couldn't stand to watch me win, so you had to take me out."

"Oh, fuck you, Ben. As if I would sacrifice my own race just so I could ruin yours. Moron."

"Oh yeah, then how do you explain my car tumbling down the track then?"

"Your terrible driving skills?"

One moment Liam was standing, and then he wasn't. In a flash, Liam was sprawled across the concrete, with Ben stood above him, his jaw flexing as he rubbed his fist.

Oh fuck, did he just... punch Liam?

Liam was back on his feet almost instantly, anger radiating from his eyes as he grabbed Ben by the collar. He was larger than Ben by nearly four inches, but Ben wasn't backing down as he pushed at Liam's chest in an effort to get free.

"What the fuck is wrong with the two of you?" I pushed between the two drivers, my gaze never leaving Ben's. John, Liam's physiotherapist, quickly grabbed Liam's shoulder and yanked him backward. The tension in the air was palpable as I continued to glare at Ben.

"Ben, get it together, fans are going to see this," I loudly whispered to him, my face mere inches from his.

"Better watch your back, Liam. Not even your cheating ass can stop me from winning this championship!"

"Oh, don't worry, Benny-boy. I'll be sure to look *behind me* next weekend after I win the race." Ben went to lunge at him again, but fortunately, John had enough sense to pull Liam out of Ben's reach, instead opting to drag his friend down the passageway and into the Wilmington garage before either Ben or Liam could make another move.

"Ben, what the fuck is wrong with you?"

"I fucking hate that prick, Poppy. He did it on purpose."

"I don't thi-" The look on Ben's face told me not to finish that sentence, and after the day we'd both had, I decided fighting with my best friend wasn't worth it.

"Let's get you home."

As we made our way out of the garage and back to Ben's car, I saw Liam off in the distance. Our eyes met from across the way, and in that moment, I could have sworn I saw an apology flash across his face. I gave him a curt nod and then climbed into the driver's seat of Ben's Mercedes.

Chapter One

POPPY

2022 SEASON

"Alright, Poppy," I heard Ben call out to me as he poked his head into my hotel room, a huge smile on his face. "You ready to head out?"

"So much for knocking, eh, Ben?" I couldn't help but chuckle at Ben and Elise, his girlfriend, as they both poked just their heads into my room.

"Since when do I have to knock?" Ben scoffed as he took a seat on my hotel room's bed, shoving a biscuit I had left out on the coffee table into his mouth.

"Since you walked in on me and Nick last year! The poor guy was so embarrassed he basically fled the room. He still can't look me in the eye…!"

Elise gasped, a wide look of horror on her face as she gave her boyfriend a playful slap. "Ben, how could you?"

"What? Poppy can do better than him anyway." I just rolled my eyes at his insistence, grabbing my purse as I gave myself one last look in my mirror, a look that earned me a wolf whistle from my two friends.

"Looking hot tonight, Poppy!" Elise exclaimed as she

grabbed my arms, forcing me to give her a twirl. "Where have you been hiding this dress... and this *body*? You're going to have all of the drivers *salivating* over you tonight."

"They had better not..." I heard a gruff voice mutter behind me. *Ben, ever the protective brother.* Even though we hadn't been born siblings, our families had essentially raised us like we were twins.

"And why not?" Elise challenged her boyfriend, eyes determined.

"Because Poppy can do better than an F1 dri-"

Before he could finish his sentence, Elise cut in, "Think carefully about those words, Benjamin."

"Judging by Liam's guest list and the number of influencers who seemed to have made the cut, I don't think any of the drivers will actually be interested in *me*..." The annoyed look on Elise's face told me that my self-deprecating joke had not landed.

"Pfft, like F1's first female racing engineer to win the World Driver's Championship isn't a hot catch!" Elise scoffed as she waved me over to the door, still giving Ben a frustrated glare. He gave her a quick apologetic kiss, before closing the hotel room door behind us, motioning for us to head to the elevator.

"You sure it's okay I'm coming?"

"Yeah, Liam said to invite you personally, according to Charlie."

"Oh...?" Elise asked, the corner of her lips slowly teasing up into a curve.

"Don't get any ideas," Ben scolded. Judging by the wiggling eyebrows on Elise's face, I knew my friend was already planning my wedding to F1's most notorious bachelor and playboy.

If Liam Fitzgerald was a character in one of my smutty historical romance novels, he undoubtedly would be King of the Rakes. I didn't know much about the Wilmington driver – *besides his good luck and overly charming personality* – but I was itching to finally have a night off from the team, and I couldn't help but let my curiosity get the better of me.

"So, you going to be civil to Liam tonight or are we still harboring a grudge from last year?" Ben just clenched his jaw at my question, a move that reminded me how bad he was at poker. No matter how hard he tried, Ben was an open book when it came to his feelings.

"I agreed to go to the party, didn't I?"

"Baby steps," Elise whispered to me, and I winked back at her, knowing that she and Charlie had played an instrumental role in getting Ben to agree to attend Liam's party.

When we arrived, we were greeted by a lot of familiar faces – drivers, race engineers, and strategists were all gathered at Liam's – *rather large* – Monaco apartment. Champagne was overflowing from the makeshift bar that I could see at the back of the house, and the guests seemed to have indulged in several bottles already.

"Poppy!" I heard a name call out across the way. I turned to see Charlie waving me over, two glasses of champagne in his hand. I signaled to Ben and Elise that I would be back, then padded over to my old friend. During our karting days, Charlie and I had been good friends. When I went to university, we drifted apart, but now that he was Wilmington's newest driver, the two of us had spent some time catching up. I knew it was partially because Wilmington had made it quite clear that they were interested in hiring me, but I was glad to have his company nonetheless.

"Poppy, I wanted to introduce you to my teammate Liam," he grinned. "Hey, Liam!" Charlie called out to the Australian driver. "Here's that incredibly smart, talented, sexy engineer I was telling you about."

As soon as I made eye contact with Liam, I felt a warmth

go through my traitorous body. Ogling my best friend's biggest rival probably shouldn't have been on my to-do list this evening, but as Liam continued to saunter over to us, I somehow forgot all of the reasons I was supposed to hate the Australian driver. Liam Fitzgerald was undoubtedly the most attractive driver on the grid. At a solid 6'1, the man was a thick build of muscle and athleticism that had all the women in the paddock swooning every time he walked by. I felt a blush creep over my cheeks, but kept my mouth in a straight line, not wanting to show my child-like excitement that Charlie had discussed me with another driver, especially one as handsome as Liam Fitzgerald.

Part of me wondered if Liam remembered me from that day in Brazil last year, remembered me getting between him and Ben, but judging by his casual smile and gleaming eyes, if he did, he wasn't planning on bringing it up. Charlie gave me a sly smirk, but said nothing; he had clearly seen the hint of excitement on my face, which I returned with a knowing glare, begging my friend not to give me away.

"Well, if it isn't the woman of the hour, the woman I keep hearing about from Charlie," Liam gasped, putting his hands in the air as if he was pretending to fangirl over me. "If I had a pound coin for every time Charlie threatened to *steal you* over to Wilmington, I'd be able to buy a second house in Monaco," he joked – *and partially bragged*.

"I don't think Charlie can *afford* to bring me over to Wilmington," I quipped, earning me a friendly shove from my friend.

"Everyone has a number," Charlie scoffed. He wasn't completely wrong, Wilmington had thrown out a few big numbers at me last year.

"Well unfortunately for Wilmington, I don't think I'd look good in the color plum, even if it is one of my favorite fruits." Charlie let out a pretend gasp at my statement – as if he didn't constantly complain about the team colors every chance he got.

"Shame, it'd be nice to have some more eye candy around the Wilmington garage. I'm really holding the field on my own in that department." Liam gave me a not-so-subtle wink, a move that sent another volt of electricity straight down to my core.

Get it together, Poppy. You're practically drooling over a man just because he winked at you.

"It's for the best. I don't think Wilmington could handle *two* attractive people working there anyway," I said in a sultry voice that – *quite frankly* – didn't sound like mine – *but apparently had been.* As a blush crept over Liam's face, I knew I had caught him off guard with my comment.

Before he could return the favor, I raised my glass. "Definitely time for a refill. Nice to meet you, Liam." And with that I sauntered off towards the bar, slightly shocked at my brazen flirting in front of my friends and peers. I wasn't usually so bold with my flirting, especially with another driver, but something about Liam made me comfortable – and my desire to challenge him just rose to the top.

As I sat at the makeshift bar, waiting for my drink, Elise reappeared, a huge smile on her face. "Umm, what was that?" She quirked an eyebrow up at me, her face latent with inquiry and way too much excitement.

"Honestly? I have absolutely no idea..." I chuckled as embarrassment began to wash over me.

"If I didn't know any better, I'd say you were flirting with a certain Australian Wilmington driver."

"Please don't tell Ben, he'll be furious," I begged, giving Elise the biggest puppy dog eyes I could muster.

"But if I don't tell Ben, he can't help me with my secret plan to get you and Liam together!"

"Not so secret if you tell one of the victims," I replied

dryly. "And something tells me Ben would rather bite off his own arm than watch me date an F1 driver, especially Liam. In case you haven't noticed, after the little... incident... last year, they're not exactly friends. Or speaking to each other." Ben might have won the championship the following race, but that didn't mean he was ready to let go of his grudge.

"I don't know what his deal is," she bemoaned. "I get you're like a sister to him, but he's gotta loosen up with the protective bullshit." As if on cue, Ben flashed us both a smile over from his corner of the room, which we both returned, me more so than Elise. "I'll think of something..."

"No, Elise, really it's fine. I don't need to add being turned down by one of the hottest F1 drivers to my bucket list."

"You know, I really hate when you do that," she mumbled.

"What?"

"I hate when you put yourself down. You're the first female racing engineer to win a championship and at the age of twenty-seven, no less. You're a fucking catch, Poppy. You just need to see that." I went to say something back to my friend, but I couldn't find the words as Elise marched back to Ben's side.

The following morning I woke up with not one, but three text messages on my phone. Confused, as it was only 8 a.m. and almost everyone I knew was guaranteed to be hungover, I opened my phone and, to my surprise, the texts were from an unknown number.

> Unknown: Hey, I hope this is okay. I got your number from Charlie. It's Liam, btw.

> Liam: I just wanted to say that I enjoyed meeting you tonight, and I was kind of hoping I'd maybe see you again at the paddock next week.
>
> Liam: I now realize that was a slightly stupid thing to say... of course you'll be there... you're Ben's race engineer... so umm, yeah, I guess I will see you next week.

I read my phone with utter disbelief, re-reading the texts several times. Liam had asked for my number from Charlie? *Why?* I immediately texted Melly, Charlie's girlfriend, to see if I could get any gossip out of her.

> Poppy: So, Liam asked Charlie for my number?
>
> Melly: Did he? Omg, let me ask Charlie.
>
> Poppy: Don't wake him for this!
>
> Melly: I cannot possibly think of a better reason to wake up Charlie than to get gossip about your new BOYFRIEND.
>
> Poppy: I'll be patiently waiting.

Lies. Nothing about my body language screamed patient.

> Melly: Okay, yes, Charlie did give him your number. He said Liam mentioned something about wanting to ask you an engineering question. I told him that was total bullshit and tried to press him for more, but he insisted that was all he got out of Liam. Sorry I can't be of more help, babe, but if you want, I'd be happy to invite you over to the Wilmington hospitality suite... you know in case you "accidentally" wanted to run into Liam.

I laughed at Melly's text. I secretly wanted to take her up on that offer, but I knew the professionalism of that was incredibly low. I wasn't a middle school girl, and I needed to stick to my own garage – not wander around competitors' garages ogling drivers who didn't work for my team.

> Poppy: Thanks, love, but best I stick to the Rennen garage in Bahrain.

Melly: <3

A knock on my door caused me to look up from my phone, and I threw it on the bed as I wrapped myself in my robe, heading towards the door to open it for whatever gremlin had managed to crawl out of bed this early in the morning.

"Morning, Pops!" The high-pitched, happy tone took me by surprise as I stood dumbfounded, staring at Ben, who was holding two cups of coffee.

"Be-Ben... its 8 a.m. on a Saturday. No offense but... what the fuck?" Ben just grinned in response, shoving one of the coffees into my hands.

"Vanilla Latte with oat milk," he announced as he plopped himself down on my couch.

"Sure... make yourself at home." I quickly shut the door and joined my friend on the couch.

"So, you have a good time last night?"

"Yes, did you?" Ben nodded in response as he took another sip of coffee, and I could see that he was stalling as he slowly sipped his coffee.

"Ben, just say what you want to say. Watching you debate what to say is worse than whatever you have to say."

"I saw you talking with Liam last night."

"Ben–"

"Look," he interrupted, putting his hand up in defense. "I chatted to Charlie this morning on our run, and he told me about your... interaction. I just.... Liam is bad news, Poppy. You know that."

"Ben, I had one conversation with Liam yesterday." Judging by the way Ben was shifting in his seat, I knew the sternness in my voice had surprised him. "I hardly think one *slightly flirty* conversation warrants this *awkward* talk."

"I just don't want you to get hurt, that's all. He's not only an asshole, but I've heard the stories of how Liam treats women...They call him *"Lead-You-On Liam"* for a reason. You deserve better than that."

"Your opinion and concern is duly noted, Ben, but I can assure you... Liam Fitzgerald has zero interest in me, okay. Now dear God let's drop it, hmm?"

"Fine, fine..." Ben sighed into his coffee.

I knew that wasn't the end of the conversation, but for now, Ben had put it to rest as I turned on the television, opting for some morning cartoons to fill the awkward silence between us.

The Bahrain pre-season testing quickly came, and before I knew it, we were back on the Rennen F1 jet, flying to the Middle Eastern track. Ben and I spent the majority of the flight reviewing changes to the car the team had made back in England. One of the things I loved the most about Ben was his proclivity to immediately understand the engineering terms I threw at him. If Ben didn't know, he asked, and he remembered.

As soon as the driver's press conference was done, both Ben and Charlie came sprinting over.

"Hey Poppy, wanna do lunch with me and Ben in an hour? Would be nice to have a little break and catch up the three of us?"

"I don't know... Ben and I have a lot to do before free practice." I gave Ben a pointed look, which he aptly ignored as he shrugged.

"Come on, Pop, we've gone over everything a million times."

"Fine, fine. A quick lunch, though!"

"Excellent!" Charlie clapped his hands together, and while his face looked calm and collected, there was an unmistakable twinkle in his eyes that I knew should have had me worried.

As soon as 12 p.m. rolled around, I found Charlie waiting for me and Ben outside of the F1 VIP suites. As the host walked us over to our reserved table, I immediately wished that I had made a greater effort with my hair and makeup this morning.

There, seated at the table waiting for us, was none other than Liam Fitzgerald, F1's most eligible bachelor, at least according to the F1 gossip site that I secretly scrolled through at night.

As soon as I saw Liam, I grabbed Charlie's arm, pulling him back into me as Ben cautiously approached the reserved table, an annoyed look on his face as he was clearly trying to figure out why Liam was there. To my relief, Ben sat down and immediately pulled out his phone as Liam did the same, both pretending to be disinterested and unbothered by the other's presence.

"Didn't know Liam would be joining us for lunch," I accused.

"Why? Does that bother you?" Charlie had a pleased smirk on his face, and I knew he was feeling very satisfied with himself. His voice was cool and collected, but it was clear I'd been caught flirting with the Australian driver the other night.

"Charlie, I am barely wearing any makeup, and I am basically covered in engine grease. I cannot have lunch with Liam," I said sternly. Charlie just snickered, grabbing me by the arm as he dragged me to the table before I could continue my protest.

"I don't see why that would matter... I thought you weren't interested in Liam." His stupid smirk told me the bastard was enjoying this way too much.

"Hey! Look who it is!" Liam exclaimed, and I could see a look of relief flash over Liam's face as Charlie and I approached the table.

As he greeted me, Liam opened his arms and gave me a hug that felt like we had known each other for years. I returned the hug – *rather shyly* – and then turned back to Charlie, giving him a small death stare as we took our seats.

"So, how are things at Wilmington?" I asked Liam once our food had been delivered.

"Fine, brakes are a little rough, but hoping we get some better advancements before the first race of the season."

Damn Liam and his sexy Australian accent. It was hard to pay attention to what he was saying as I watched him speak. His awkward laugh was followed by two adorable dimples on either side of his face, a perfect frame for his ridiculously attractive smile.

"You know, if we had a certain engineer on our team, I'm sure we'd be able to figure it out quicker," Liam chuckled, throwing me a cheeky wink and a devilish grin.

Before I could pull myself out of my head and respond, Ben cut in, and I knew from his face that he was incredibly annoyed with this lunch. "Not a chance, boys, Poppy and I have a few more WDCs to win over at Rennen." Ben put his arm around my shoulder as he smiled brightly, although his death grip told me exactly how he felt about this exchange.

I just grinned in response as I shoved Ben off me. "Ben's right. Plus, as I keep telling Charlie, I don't think I'd look very good in plum."

"Nonsense, I can't think of a single color that you wouldn't look *divine* in... but if you really insist that plum isn't your color, *nothing* is also an option." I felt Ben tense up next to me as he choked on part of his salad at Liam's compliment, but I just *casually* rolled my eyes as I tried to push down the blush that I knew had completely taken over my face.

There's that charming, suave playboy everyone is always talking about.

I could tell that Ben was about to say something that would be plenty rude, but before he could snap back at the Australian, his phone rang, and he quickly checked his messages.

"Shit, sorry Poppy, I gotta head to this stupid VIP event right now. Mind getting the rest of my salad to go?"

"Of course, no problem."

"Charlie, make sure Poppy gets back to the garage unscathed, hmm?" Judging by the scoff that Liam let out, the subtle message behind Ben's words was... *not that subtle*.

After our lunches were finished, Charlie immediately

stood up from the table. "Right, well, I've got... um... something to do. See you later, yeah?"

"Charlie, get the fuck back over here!" I demanded, but he just waved me off as I scoffed in disbelief.

"And then there were two..." Liam grinned. For a moment, I almost wondered if he and Charlie had planned this. "Fancy a little walk around the paddock to burn off those calories?" I opened my mouth to protest, but staring back at me was probably the world's biggest smile, and I just didn't have the heart to say no to his soft curly brown hair and bright green eyes. As soon as Ben's salad was packed up, Liam motioned for us to head towards the exit.

"So, Mr. Fitzgerald, I heard a rumor that you had engineering questions," I teased, hinting back to the texts he had sent me two weeks ago. Liam's cheeks went slightly red as he chuckled with what looked like... *embarrassment?*

"Yes, I did, but the lovely engineer I texted never responded, so I had to ask my own race engineer, who is not nearly as exciting... or as good-looking." As he gave me a little wink and a nudge, a rush of electricity shot through my body at his touch, and I tried to hide the blush that I knew hadn't really left my face since we had started lunch.

"What a bitch for not responding to you. You should get that engineer fired." I winked at him with as much mischievousness as I could muster, and Liam let out a loud laugh that made my heart warm. As much as I hated to admit it, chatting with Liam felt natural. He had a certain air about him that could make anyone feel comfortable.

"You know, I think you have a point. If I get her fired, then she'll have to come work for *me* over at Wilmington," he mused, looking up into the sky as if he was asking a deity up above to grant his wish. I jokingly shoved his shoulders, pulling him back down to earth.

"I don't know, Liam, I heard that she doesn't flirt with

coworkers, so you might want to rethink that plan, but, if you stay on her good side, she might consider answering any other questions you have for her."

"Really? Well then, I'm just going to have to stay on her good side, can't be angering the paddock's most *desirable* engineer." It was the way he said desirable that had my cheeks heating up. His phrase made it sound like I was desirable because I had won the World Driver's Championship with Ben, but the look on his face – *and his tone* – said that desirable clearly meant something else.

When we reached the Rennen F1 garage, I immediately saw Ben outside, impatiently waiting for me. As soon as he saw me walk up with Liam, he practically ran over, a vexed expression on his face.

"Poppy, you alright?" The urgency in Ben's voice earned him a glare from Liam.

"Sorry, Ben, was just telling Poppy what it's like to work with a *real* racing team. " I gave Liam a jab in his ribs, but he just grinned at me smugly.

"Oh yeah, did you find one that would hire you?" Ben smirked, and I immediately got in the middle of Ben and Liam as I shoved the leftover salad into Ben's chest.

"We went on a track walk to get some fresh air. Let's get back to the strategy review, hmm?"

"Better finish that salad, Benny-boy; you're looking snug in that racing suit these days!" Liam snickered. He bent down and gave me a kiss on the cheek, before strolling off towards his garage. Ben just flicked him off as he turned to me, but I just shooed him away as I headed to my office, not interested in getting yet another one of Ben's lectures.

Chapter Two
POPPY

These interactions with Liam carried on for several more months. We would text throughout the week – Liam sending me silly engineering questions that he could clearly get answered at Wilmington, me responding with equally long and obnoxious engineering answers.

It had become our thing.

But as the texting and phone calls became more frequent, it was starting to become even more difficult to hide my friendship with Liam from Ben. During race weekends, Liam and I would meet for coffee in his hotel room or enjoy late-night snacks as we watched silly cartoons together – whatever moments we could steal away for ourselves without Ben knowing. And while our interactions had been filled with plenty of flirting, they had always remained platonic.

Every part of me knew I shouldn't want Liam, that our love was doomed before it had even begun, and yet even with that knowledge, I couldn't stop spending every free moment thinking about him.

A ding from my phone pulled me out of my thoughts,

and as soon as I read the texts, I couldn't stop a giddy smile from forming on my face.

> Liam: You got any plans for the Monaco Driver's Gala?

> Poppy: You mean besides not going?

> Liam: Oh... you don't want to go?

> Poppy: Liam, it's a joke. They don't exactly invite racing engineers to these fancy VIP events, silly.

> Liam: They do if they're a date of a handsome race car driver.

> Poppy: Oh yeah, you know of a handsome driver looking for a date?

> Liam: In fact... I do!

My stomach dropped as I read his text. Was Liam trying to set me up with one of the other drivers?

> Poppy: Oh, well, umm, yeah I'm free if they're asking, I guess?

> Liam: And what if that driver asking is me? Would you still say yes?

> Poppy: Liam Fitzgerald, are you asking me to go on a date with you?

> Liam: Only if you plan on saying yes... if you plan on saying no, then no... because I don't think my ego can handle being turned down the paddock's most desirable engineer ;-)

There he was with that word again – *desirable*.

I looked around the garage, making sure no one was staring at me. I knew my face made me look like a kid in a candy store. Unfortunately, I immediately made eye contact with Ben, who gave me a solemn, pissed-off look as he went back to the notes he was reviewing with our strategist. Ben had been in a mood all morning, and I was starting to think I knew why.

> Poppy: I should probably ask Ben.

> Liam: Charlie told him I was going to ask during the driver's press conference this morning.

Ahh, there is was.
The reason Ben had been icing me out all morning.
Fucking toddler with his tantrums.
I knew exactly what Ben thought about this situation. He'd told me over and over again that the other drivers were off limits, that *'I could do better'* as he liked to bemoan. A part of my heart knew I should listen, but as I got to know Liam, another part, the part that was longing for something fun and fresh, started to win out.

> Poppy: Explains why he was in a bad mood this morning.

> Liam: So...?

> Poppy: Sure, it'll be fun.

> Liam: That's the spirit! I took the liberty of having a little something sent to your room... enjoy.

The first thing I noticed when I walked into my hotel room was the most beautiful dress lying on top of my duvet.

"Of course, it's fucking plum," I grumbled as I picked up the dress, admiring the elegant beadwork around the edges.

Poppy: Plum? Really?

Liam: I wanted to put that theory of you not looking good in plum to the test.

Poppy: I'm afraid you're about to be very disappointed then.

Liam: Don't worry, if you don't look good in it, we can always test out that you wearing nothing theory.

Poppy: Cheeky bastard.

I packed up my dress and crossed over into Ben and Elise's room, where a hair and makeup stylist was waiting for us. Even though he was icing me out, Ben had very kindly offered to let Elise and I get ready in their room. He had even offered to pay for the experience, as a thank you for all my hard work – but I knew it was because Elise had told him too.

"So, Poppy, I didn't know you and Liam had gotten so... close," she teased as she wiggled her eyebrows. "I thought Ben was going to explode when Charlie told him that Liam was going to ask you."

"Tell Ben there's nothing to worry about, Liam and I are just friends. I'm sure his other date cancelled on him, and he needed someone last minute."

"There you are with all of that self-doubt again," she said pointedly as she filled up my glass with far too much champagne.

"I mean he did ask me all of six hours ago..."

"Maybe he was too nervous. I mean he must have gotten that dress well in advance. One doesn't just buy the newest Louis Vuitton collection on a whim, especially not in your size."

"If we were in any other city but Monaco, El, I'd maybe believe you." The look on her face told me she didn't appreciate the sarcasm dripping from my voice. To be fair, Monaco was probably the one place where you could get any designer dress at any point in the day.

"Whatever, Poppy. I know I won't change your mind, but just don't write him off so soon, hmm?"

"Look at you, Little Ms. Sneaky. Does Ben know you're Team Liam?"

"I know Liam and Ben have a bad... history, but at some point Ben is going to have to let it go. He won the championship last year – not Liam. I mean they used to be close... hell, you've clearly let it go."

"Yeah, well, I wasn't in a car that was turned upside down by Liam." The two of us sat there silently for a moment, and I knew she was also reliving that memory. A familiar feeling of dread began to creep up as I thought about Ben's car flipping once, twice, then a third time as it tumbled off the track.

"Well," Elise said, finally breaking the trance that we had both fallen into. "If we're going to double date, he'll have to let it go." The finality of her voice and grin on her face told me she was done discussing this – but wasn't done with her scheming.

Elise's ability to forgive and forget astounded me. Truthfully if a driver had caused my boyfriend's car to catch fire, I'm not sure I could so casually let it go, but that was the magic of Elise, why she made such a good girlfriend to a Formula 1 driver. The bad times rolled off of her so easily, and the good times were always top of mind.

As 6 p.m. rolled around, Ben finally joined us in the hotel room, his cheeks a little pink from the drinks I knew he had been having with Charlie.

"Ladies, looking lovely as always," Ben announced, giving Elise a kiss on her cheek as she finished putting on her lipstick. He eyed my dress and his face fell flat as soon as he registered the color. After a double take, he finally walked over to me, a grin now replacing the stoic frown that had been on his face just moments earlier.

"You look beautiful, Poppy," he said as he pulled me into a hug. "Don't love the color..." he added, a hint of annoyance in his voice, "but it'll be nice to have you there, even if it means you going with *Liam*."

"Must we do this now," Elise groaned, giving her boyfriend a pointed look that told me they had spent the entire afternoon discussing this very topic. Ben just nodded, plastering back on his smile as he held out his arm for Elise and me.

As the three of us made our way downstairs, I saw Liam waiting for me outside the hotel lobby, looking as dashing as ever. Ben immediately noticed Liam, and before either of us could say something, he walked up to the Australian, poking a finger in his chest.

"If you hurt her, Liam, I swear to God I will run you off this fucking track and into the barriers this weekend, understood?"

"Aye, aye, Benny-boy," Liam chuckled. At the mention of his old nickname, Ben's face reddened as he clenched his jaw. I shot Liam an all-knowing glare, begging for him to stop before he dug himself in any deeper. Ben took a deep breath as he tried to compose himself, before turning away, deciding it was time for him to make his exit.

As soon as Ben and Elise were out of earshot, I shoved

Liam's shoulder. "Really? You just *had* to get under his skin, huh?"

"Sorry... it's just too easy sometimes!"

Liam and I's seats were at a table with several other drivers and their girlfriends, most of whom I had never been properly introduced to. The nerves from the occasion were making my hand sweat profusely, but Liam grabbed my hand anyway and led us to the table, smiling at everyone we passed with his ridiculously beautiful pearly-white smile.

"Hello everyone, I'd like to introduce you to Poppy." The group smiled at me warmly, and I took my spot between Liam and Arthur, the previous year's Formula 1 champion before Ben had taken it off him.

"So, you are the famous engineer that Liam cannot stop talking about?" Arthur winked at Liam, and I could have sworn he almost blushed.

"If you mean, am I the engineer Liam and Charlie keep trying to steal away from Ben, then yes."

"I mean, I love my race engineer like a brother, but if Rennen ever let you go, I'd hire you in a second – so I can't say I blame them," Arthur gushed, much to my surprise. Arthur seemed so emotionless in the paddock, always so levelheaded.

As the main courses started to come out, so did what felt like mountains of champagne. While I was hopeful that the food would sober me up, I felt like every time I started to get my wits about me, another round of champagne was brought out to the table. Fortunately for me, everyone was starting to get a little sloshed by the last course, Liam included.

When the dessert finally arrived, I felt Liam's hand drift to my leg, his thumb gently rubbing circles as the inside of his fingers started to *very lightly* scrape up and down the inside of my thigh. My breath hitched, and out of the corner of my eye, I saw Liam smirk. I tried to continue to listen to whatever Henri was droning on about, but it was incredibly hard as Liam's large hand kept stroking the inside of my thigh, ever so lightly, never progressing up to where I was beginning to want them.

Oh the motherfucker wants to play ... fine, two can play at this game.

I'm not sure if it was all the booze that gave me confidence, but I silently excused myself and quickly went to the bathroom. I took a moment to think about how I could get revenge on Liam, and then it hit me. Underneath my beautiful purple dress I had worn a plum lingerie set. I, truthfully, didn't expect the night to end with my dress on the floor, but something about wearing a rival team's color lingerie felt incredibly exciting.

I slipped off my panties and put them in my purse. When I returned to the table, I took the plum-colored thong and discreetly slid it into Liam's jacket pocket, which was hanging on the back of his chair.

> Poppy: Put a little surprise in your jacket.

Liam's phone was in his pocket, and I could hear it vibrate immediately after I sent the sneaky text. He quirked an eyebrow at me as if to ask if I had sent that text. I just smirked at him and turned back to the table's conversation. Out of the corner of my eye I could see Liam checking his phone under the table, his eyes all of a sudden going wide. His hands reached for his jacket pocket, and I could tell the moment he felt my lacy thong, because he swallowed thickly.

As Liam shifted in his seat uncomfortably, Arthur leaned over.

"Everything alright there, mate?"

The Wilmington driver shook his head yes as he shifted a little closer to me in his seat. "Just felt a little... warm all of a sudden," he replied, a big smile on his face. "Must be all this champagne." Arthur nodded, raising his glass as he clinked it with Liam's.

A few more moments went by, and Liam still hadn't said anything to me, instead opting to continue his conversation with Henri about the weekend's press events. Just as I started to have doubts about my earlier move, I felt Liam's hands on my thigh again – this time much higher, as if he was trying to see if I had actually taken my thong off.

As his fingers slowly crept up to their destination, I could see his eyes go wide when he realized that, *yes, straight-laced Poppy had actually taken off her underwear.* I threw Liam a confident smirk, still keeping my eyes on Henri who was telling a funny story about his time working with Charlie.

What I hadn't factored in, I soon realized, was what Liam was going to do once he clocked that I wasn't wearing any underwear. Truthfully, after several glasses of champagne, I had sort of forgotten myself, but the thought excited me now.

Maybe he'll take me back to his room and punish me for being so daring in public.

Liam's hand began to move up my thigh and soon, the tips of his fingers were ghosting my core, ever so teasingly. I gasped just a tad, loud enough only for Liam to hear – his eyes were intently on me as I continued to look at anything but him. Soon his fingers began to rub a little harder as they finally made contact with the apex of my thighs.

Oh fuck, is Liam actually going to finger me under the table?

I began to panic – both horrified at the thought of him

doing it, but also desperate for him to continue. Liam continued to skillfully rub exactly where I needed him most under the table, transitioning from feather light touches to hard circles. I was starting to tumble into a fit of pleasure, doing everything in my power to keep a straight face, but based on the smirk on Liam's face, he knew I was close.

Fortunately for me, the other couples at the table had decided to go dance, leaving just Liam and me at the table. As if on cue, he pushed one finger into me as his thumb rubbed my clit, and I could feel my body start to reach that high that I hadn't experienced in far too long.

"Shh, princess, don't want anyone to know our secret," Liam whispered as I tried to even out my breathing.

"Hey Liam, you and Poppy gonna join us over here?" Arthur called out, and Liam immediately pulled his hands from under my skirt. Arthur looked at my flushed face and turned to Liam, his eyes narrowing into slits, and I knew he was trying to figure what was going on.

Liam casually smiled as he replied, "Nah, I think I gotta get this one home – you know our engineers, always up early in the morning prepping the cars that we break." Arthur chuckled, clearly not believing Liam's pathetic lie.

"And since when has Ben ever wrecked a car... at least one that you weren't responsible for, " Arthur teased. I could feel Liam tense, but he just as quickly relaxed as he awkwardly chuckled back at Arthur's *inappropriate* joke, waving off his old friend and former teammate. As soon as Arthur left the table, Liam turned back to me, his face incredibly smug as he eyed the blush on my face that I was unable to hide.

"Come on, baby girl, let's get you back to the hotel, hmmm?" Liam whispered in my ear.

I nodded in agreement and quickly collected my things

from the table, my legs still a little wobbly. As we reached the exit, I heard a familiar voice call out to us.

"Where are you two heading off to so early?" Charlie called over, waving for us to come closer. Liam let out a little sigh in frustration, and it took me a moment to realize why he had placed me in front of him. I felt a slight bulge against my back, and I immediately knew what he was trying to hide. A rush of warmth spread through my body as he leaned in closer.

Was Liam Fitzgerald, F1's most desirable bachelor, as into this as I was?

"Poppy is pretty tired, so I'm going to take her back to the hotel," Liam replied simply, and I knew from the finality of his voice that he was hoping the conversation would end at that.

Before Charlie could reply, Melly butt in, giving Charlie a glare, "Get some sleep, Poppy, good to see you!" She made her boyfriend turn around as she wiggled her eyebrows suggestively at me, and I sent her a sly grin as a thank you.

My phone vibrated, and I quickly eyed my texts from Ben, rolling my eyes at his eager attempt to get me away from Liam.

> Ben: Is that you leaving?
>
> Ben: Do you need me to bring you back?

Not this time, Ben.

I hadn't had sex in what felt like an eternity, and here I had one of the sexiest men in the paddock ready and willing to give me a night of fun that I so desperately craved.

Fuck it, I'll deal with the fallout from Ben later.

> Poppy: Tell Ben I'm fine.

Elise: GET IT GIRL.

As we walked outside, Liam ushered us into the cab that was already waiting for us. He got us both buckled in and then grabbed my neck, pulling my face towards his.

"I've been wanting to do this for so long," he whispered before he kissed me with such passion and force that I was pushed back up against the side of the car. I took my hands and wrapped them around his neck and upper back, trying to pull him as close to me as possible. He broke free for a moment, both of us gasping for air in the process. He smiled at me, that million-dollar smile, and I knew I was done for.

"You sure you wanna come back to mine?" He asked in a light whisper. For the first time that evening, I saw Liam's confidence waver. His voice was low and velvety, his hands shaking slightly as he tucked a stray strand of hair behind my ear. His gaze lingered on mine for the briefest of moments before he bit his lip nervously. I let out a small laugh before leaning in to kiss him. He smiled against my mouth, and I nodded in agreement.

"Don't go soft on me now, Liam."

The ride to his hotel was incredibly short, and I felt horrible for the driver who had to endure the two of us in his back seat, even if I knew that Liam had given him a very large tip. We rushed up the stairs, holding hands lightly as we waited for the elevator to take us to the top floor. When the elevator rang, Liam grabbed my hand and dragged me to his suite, eagerly opening the door with his hotel key.

As soon as his hotel room door closed, I felt my back being pushed against the wall, and Liam was kissing me again, this time a little more slowly, but with as much gusto as before. He pulled my hips towards him and turned me, slowly guiding me back towards his bed. My back hit the cozy comforter, and Liam pounced on top of me, placing his thigh in between my legs as he pressed it against my core.

I sighed into his mouth, reveling in his touch. Liam slid his hands up my dress, rubbing them up and down the sides of my waist. After a few moments, he flipped me over and I felt the back of my dress being unzipped.

"I think we should get this off of you, don't you agree, princess?" All I could do at that moment was nod, too wrapped up in his sultry voice to possibly utter a word of my own.

Liam unzipped my dress and pulled it off of me, leaving me in just my lacy bra. Slowly, Liam flipped me over, his eyes raking up and down my body as he winked at me, making me giggle like a schoolgirl whose biggest crush had finally given her some attention.

"Well damn, I never thought I would appreciate seeing a Rennen girl in plum as much as I do now, but this sight is even better than the fucking dress," he purred.

"I never thought I'd find a rival worthy of wearing such a godforsaken color."

Liam laughed – *genuinely laughed* – and then quickly whipped my bra off, much to my surprise. Before I could protest him destroying my *expensive* lingerie set, his hands were back on me, his face ghosting my lips.

"You're awfully cocky for someone completely naked in my bed," he grinned at me.

The fact that Liam was on top of me fully clothed, while I was completely naked underneath him, should not have turned me on as much as it did. I wanted to retort something cocky, but the truth was he had won that battle, and I had very little to say, so instead I reached for his belt.

While I could see Liam was still itching to be in control, he was curious. I undid his belt and buttons and slid his pants down just enough so that I could see the top of his boxers. Slowly I reached for his cock, letting my hand stroke over his incredibly hard length. I pulled down his pants a little more, and his cock sprung free – it was red and leaking with pre-cum, and it looked absolutely delicious. I looked up at him and batted my eyelashes, a silent plea to let me taste him.

Liam smirked and nodded. "Go ahead and be a good girl for me. I know you want to."

Fuck, why was that so hot?

I let my tongue slowly lick up and down his base, my hands cupping his balls and massaging them ever so gently. I could hear him hiss the moment my tongue reached his tip. I slowly put his entire cock in my mouth and bobbed up and down, slowly teasing him with each movement.

Liam grabbed the back of my head. "Stop teasing baby girl, or I'll be sure to punish you later."

While a punishment seemed more like a reward from Liam than something to be feared, I obliged his command and began to bob up and down with more speed than before, increasing my pace each time I went back down, slowly letting him hit the back of my throat. As I could feel Liam began to reach his high, he stopped me, pulling my head back as he guided me back onto the bed.

"While this has been amazing, princess, I want to feel all of you, be inside of you," he grunted, trying to regain composure. Liam sat up on the back of the bed against the headboard and placed me on his lap. I felt him reach over to his bedside table and pull out a condom, which he slid on quickly. He slowly reached to his shirt collar and began to untie his tie. I raised an eyebrow at him, curious as to what he had in mind.

He just smirked at me and asked, "Do you trust me?" I nodded in response, but he motioned for me to utter the words.

"Yes," I rasped.

"Good. Now put your hands behind your back."

I felt him guide my wrists to my back as he slowly tied his suit tie around my wrists. As soon as my hands were bound, Liam dragged me onto his lap so that my back and wrists were against his chest, the two of us facing the huge floor-length mirror that sat in front of the bed.

"Want to feel all of you, princess, you okay with that?"

I nodded my silent – but incredibly eager – consent and Liam lifted my hips and slowly set me onto his cock, letting each inch deliciously fill me as I continued to sink down, bottoming out after what felt like a lifetime.

In that moment, I knew that Liam had ruined me for all other men, but I couldn't find it in myself to care.

As he buried himself deep inside of me, I moaned what can only be described as the loudest moan I had ever uttered, resting my head in the crook of his neck. With all the teasing and pent-up frustration from earlier, Liam had prepared me for his cock, so I was more than ready for him.

"Fuck, Liam, that feels so...so good," I gritted out, trying to rock my hips back and forth, desperate to feel even more of him. Liam put his hands on my hips and stopped me, and I could see his smug face in the mirror.

"You move when I tell you to, baby girl, understood? You don't come until I give you permission. Until you beg for it." Part of me wanted to argue back, tell him I didn't take orders from men, and I certainly didn't beg them for things, a thought that was quickly thrown out of my mind as soon as Liam started to rub the apex of my thighs.

Fuck it, I thought. *Everyone's a feminist until a 6'1, incredibly sexy athlete ties you up and demands you to beg for him.*

Liam began to lift my hips up and down on his cock, silently reveling in the incredible feeling of our bodies being joined. The slow movement felt incredibly sensual and romantic – something that I wasn't used to. My last boyfriend had been more of a quick in-and-out sort of fuck, but Liam was nothing like him. His movements were slow and deliberate, as if his only focus in life was making sure I felt every inch of him, that he felt every inch of me.

After several more thrusts, I could feel myself start to come apart, my moans getting louder as he reached his hand down to where I wanted them most, gently stroking my folds.

"Liam... I'm going to come. Need to..." I begged, doing everything within myself to hold it together, to be the good girl that Liam wanted me to be.

"Not yet, princess," he said smoothly, although I could feel him pick up his pace. His thrusts began to feel more erratic, and I could tell that he was getting closer. I don't know if it was the fact that I was completely naked and tied up plus the fact that he was fully clothed, with only his cock free from his pants, but I was starting to very quickly fall into a deep ecstasy, one that I couldn't fight off, no matter how much I wanted to wait for Liam.

"Pl-Please."

"You can beg better than that, Poppy?"

A part of me didn't want to beg, didn't want to give him the smug satisfaction, but that part lost out completely as soon as Liam hit a spot that sent shivers down my spine.

"Fuck... Liam..."

"Yes?" He said all too cooly. *Prick*.

"Please, Liam... fuck, please... it feels too good. Fuck, so amazing."

I could feel Liam pick up his pace as he whispered, "Go ahead, sweetheart, you've been so good for me," before placing his hand on my clit as he started to rub deep circles. Within seconds I could feel my body tumble into the most intense orgasm as I screamed – *no, chanted* – his name for everyone on the floor, perhaps the entire hotel, to hear. I could tell my orgasm triggered his, because not long after, he came with a sudden volt, grabbing onto my hips and calling out my name as he praised me for being 'such a good girl for him', letting me know 'how proud of me he was.'

Fuck me and this praise kink. With that sultry Australian accent, I was pretty sure I would do just about anything for Liam Fitzgerald.

For several minutes after, we both sat on his bed, trying to catch our breaths – me still on his lap and him still deep inside of me as I watched the two of us in the large bedroom mirror. It felt comforting to have his hands around me as they slowly trailed up and down my body, stroking gentle circles over my breasts. Once we had both calmed down from our highs, he untied my hands from behind my back, throwing his tie onto the floor as he dragged me next to him, placing my head on his chest. I felt a kiss reach my forehead before I felt him get out of bed, returning only minutes later with a washcloth and a large Wilmington t-shirt, which he slid over my head.

I opened my mouth to protest as he slipped the t-shirt over my head, but no words came out. After cleaning himself up, he crawled back into bed, now only in his boxers, and I flung myself over him, letting my head rest in the crook of his neck.

"You sure you don't want me to leave?" I asked it in such a small voice I wasn't sure if he had heard me. Now it was my confidence that was wavering.

"Oh baby girl, don't be silly, if I asked you to leave, I wouldn't be able to spend all tomorrow morning trying to convince you to be *my* race engineer," he said slyly.

Before I knew it, Liam had his hand on my thigh again, slowly stroking circles up and down it. "And I can be very convincing."

I'm in for a long night, I thought to myself, turning back to Liam as I gave him a big kiss.

Liam kept his word and the next morning, he did his best to convince me to join the Wilmington team. After another two rounds, I had to admit – the opportunity was starting to look more appealing. When my phone dinged, I heard Liam groan, insisting that I should ignore it, but I knew I couldn't avoid the rest of the world forever.

Elise: Coffee?

Poppy: Little busy now, El.

Elise: Oh, I know… it's all over Instagram!
Come over and give me the sordid details.
;-)

All over Instagram? Fuck, fuck, fuck.

I turned around to see Liam aimlessly scrolling through his phone. If he had seen any posts about us, he didn't say anything. His face was grinning as he read something on his phone.

"Um, shoot, Liam... I agreed to have coffee with Elise," I *half* lied. He turned over and grabbed me, trailing kisses down my neck as I squirmed free.

"You alright, Poppy?"

"Yeah, just don't want to be late." I immediately got up and grabbed my items, staring at the dress from last night.

Fuck, now everyone is going to know, if they don't already.

"Here." As if Liam had read my mind, he handed me a sweatshirt and a pair of his workout shorts. "Wear these back to your room. You can give them to me later," he said with a wink, and I appreciated him trying to lighten the mood. I knew he could see the anxiety on my face.

"Thanks." I gave him a weak smile and a kiss, before shoving the items on, grabbing my purse and making a beeline back to my room, where Elise was conveniently already waiting with a cup of coffee.

"Well, well, well, look what the cat dragged in," she snickered, handing me my coffee as she gave my outfit a once over.

"Thanks," I sighed, taking a seat on the couch next to her.

"Sooooo, did you have fun last night-"

"What do you mean by all over Instagram?" I cut in.

"Poppy, it was a joke. A few people saw you leave, there's a couple posts about it, nothing more."

"Fuck, fuck, fuck!" This was bad, very bad. I had told the team that I would be going with Liam to the gala, and my team had okayed it, but being caught having a one-night stand with a driver? That was not on the approved list of activities for yesterday evening.

"Poppy, what?"

"Ben is going to freak out. Ah, fuck, going to the gala with Liam was a bad idea." Panic started to fill me as I started to pace the room.

"Well, if it makes you feel any better, Ben is already freaking out," she teased. I gave her an exasperated look. As if now was the time to joke about this. "But who cares about what Ben thinks, did you have fun?" Elise asked. Easy for her to say, whenever Ben got angry at her, she was able to put on a new lingerie set and wave all of their troubles away with a magic wand.

"Ye-yes, it was fun. But-"

"No buts. You're allowed to have fun, Poppy."

"Not so sure thats true with a driver on a rival team! And

now the whole world knows... there's no way I can take that Wilmington offer now. Fuck, everyone will think that I slept my way into it."

"Did you want to take it?" Elise eyed me warily. We hadn't really discussed my other job offers because, as far as I was concerned, I was 100% dedicated to my Rennen F1 career.

"No, but..." *But I wanted it to be an option.* And now it wasn't, could never be an option. I'd never be taken seriously again.

As I looked down at my phone, I saw a link in my inbox from Melly. I clicked the link and was immediately brought to an F1 gossip account that had just posted a photo of Liam and me from last night, the two of us dancing to the live band, a huge smile on both of our faces.

If I'd known Liam would go for just anyone, I would have taken my shot with him.

How did she manage to bag Liam Fitzgerald? His last girlfriend was prettier.

Since when did Liam start taking pity dates to one of F1's biggest events?

As I read the comments, my eyes started to fill with tears. Elise immediately noticed and she grabbed my phone, setting it down on the table. "Poppy, you can't read that garbage. They do it to all the girlfriends, it doesn't matter... it's just noise."

"Easy for you to say," I scoffed.

"What's that supposed to mean?" Elise stiffened as I said the words, and I immediately regretted them.

"Nothing... just... I'm not you, Elise. I'm not cut out for this. You and the other girlfriends have skin as hard as nails. I mean fuck, I'm not even dating Liam and here I am in tears."

"It'll get bett-"

"No. Just... stop, Elise. I know you mean well, but stop. This isn't me. One night stands with my best friend's rival? What the fuck is wrong with me?" Elise said nothing as she leaned back into my sofa, taking a deep breath.

"I'm going to go have a shower. Thanks for the coffee, El." I gave her a sad smile as I made my way over to the bathroom, quickly turning on the water so that I could let it wash away the tears that were now streaming down my face.

Chapter Three

POPPY

2023 SEASON

The 2022 season had been a great success. Ben and I had achieved our second title together, and the offers from other teams were flooding in - promising me promotions, higher wages and privileges that surpassed my dreams. In spite of these tempting offers, I couldn't bring myself to abandon Rennen – or Ben. He had taken a chance on me, offering me the opportunity to become his race engineer, and deep down I felt we still had more work to do – more championships to win.

"So, I hear a rumor that Wilmington has offered you a very big number to leave Rennen," Elise said as she aimlessly scrolled through her phone, no doubt looking for an appropriate racing picture to post on her social media accounts.

"Ben really does have a big mouth," I grumbled, knowing all too well that I was about to get a lecture from Elise.

"As much as I would miss you over in the Rennen garage, that was a huge opportunity you turned down from Wilmington. The chance to sit on the panel that finalizes the Wilmington F1 car design is incredible!"

"It is," I agreed with a nod. "But I love my job at Rennen. I love sitting on the pit wall and working with Ben... there's something special about it." While Rennen hadn't offered me a spot on the car design team like Wilmington had, they had promoted me and moved me into more car design meetings, a move that told me they were thinking about my future.

"Sure, but to be on the design board, Poppy... that's amazing," Elise continued as if she hadn't heard a single word out of my mouth.

"Contrary to popular belief, Elise, I do actually work on the car design as Ben's racing engineer," I awkwardly chuckled, taking another sip of my coffee as I silently hoped that Elise would drop it.

"Sure it's cause you didn't want to see Liam every day?"

"No, Elise, I didn't turn down a world-class opportunity because of a man."

Fucking Elise with her telepathy, I moaned to myself. That wasn't *entirely* true. Liam hadn't been the reason I had declined the opportunity, but he definitely had made his way onto the con's side of the list.

"Fine, fine. Keep your secrets," she lamented. "But can you at least tell me why things seemed to fizzle out with him last year?"

"We just decided to be friends, El, nothing more."

"You two seem to be barely even be friends these days," she retorted with an all-knowing eye roll. "And that choice was... your decision?"

"A mutual one."

"Uh huh... cause Charlie told me-"

"Oh good grief, fine. It was mostly mine. Happy?" I snapped, trying to keep my frustrated tone to a minimum.

"Hey, contrary to what Ben thinks, you can date whoever you want, Pop." I just sighed as I turned back to my pastry.

"But, I still don't understand why. Liam is incredibly hot, a great racing driver, has a wicked sense of humor... oh, and did I mention how *hot* he was?"

"Several times..." I grumbled as I opened up my phone, praying that I could come up with some sort of excuse to escape this conversation.

Nothing.

"Look, after the Monaco Grand Prix Driver's Gala, we decided to be just friends. If I ever want to be taken seriously by Wilmington or other teams, sleeping with an F1 driver is *not* the way to do it. Plus, the life of an F1 driver's girlfriend... it's just not for me." I could see that Elise had taken offense to that. "The wives and girlfriends – you all are constantly analyzed, constantly being evaluated against one another. I don't exactly want to throw myself into the mix. Being compared to a bunch of beautiful models... just seems like a hit to my self-esteem that I'm not really looking for." I tried to add a joke at the end to lighten the mood, but I could see from Elise's face that she was less than impressed with my explanation.

But it was the truth, not that I had told Liam that. When Wilmington came sniffing around, offering me the job, I couldn't say yes. The idea of working with Liam Fitzgerald day in and day out seemed like a nightmare. When Liam heard about my offer from Wilmington, he begged me to take it.

While Liam had, once again, been pretty convincing after the Belgium Grand Prix last season, I declined Wilmington's offer the next day, much to his disappointment.

"I'm pretty sure it's us that should be worried, Pop, not you. Compared to you, I'm nobody. Just a name with a few hundred thousand TikTok followers."

"Now who's the one putting herself down now, hmm?" I gave Elise a little shove of encouragement.

"Fine, fine. I still don't agree with your decision, but you're a grown-ass woman who has a grown-ass job; you don't need me convincing you that you're wrong – you'll figure it out all by yourself." She stuck her tongue out at me, shoving me back a bit as we both laughed.

"Are you guys at least still friends?"

"I don't know... ever since that night in Belgium, after we slept together a second time, I felt like our friendship had taken a bit of a left turn, which I suppose I should have expected. It's not exactly what you do with someone you want to be *just friends* with..."

"Have you spoken since the season started?"

"No, my last text from him was from pre-season in February," I sighed, knowing I couldn't hide the sadness in my voice. "I miss his laughter and his jokes... but I guess we weren't much of friends before we slept together, so I guess there wasn't too much friendship to go back to."

"Well, maybe we'll catch sight of him tonight at the Silverstone party. There's still time for you guys to be... *just friends*."

"Elise Meredith Lancaster, put away your scheming mind right now or I swear to God-"

"Or you'll what, give me more empty threats." She stuck her tongue out at me as we both heard a knock at the door. Before I could answer, in walked Ben, a huge smile on his face.

"Ben, good grief, there's no point in knocking if you're going to just walk in anyway," I grumbled, eyeing the dress bag in his hand.

"I come bearing gifts... I think? Elise, is this what you wanted?" Elise quickly got up from the couch and ran over to the dress bag, quickly tearing it open as she pulled out a beautiful gold dress.

"Perfect! This was the one! Here, Poppy, you're going to wear this tonight! You'll be sure to turn heads."

As I stared at the dress Ellise had just presented to me, I couldn't help but gape at her. I didn't usually wear dresses this revealing to F1 parties, especially not gold ones. Unless you worked for the prestigious Hermes F1 Team, gold was an unspoken 'off limits' color.

"And before you complain, yes, I know it's gold, but fuck it, you're going to look fabulous in this!"

As I tried on the dress, I couldn't help but agree – I looked fucking fabulous. *Fuck it,* I thought to myself. I hadn't felt this sexy in a dress since the Monaco Grand Prix Gala last year.

Once Elise and I finished getting ready in my room, I saw Ben and Henri, Hermes F1's number one driver, walk out of the room across the hall. The boys had been drinking beers in Ben's room while we got ready in mine. When I stepped into the hallway, I saw Henri's eyes rake over my body, and I felt a pang of satisfaction.

Inviting Hermes' "golden boy" Henri to join us? What was Elise playing at?

Ben's eyes watched Henri as he smirked at the sight of my dress, but he said nothing, instead giving Elise a frustrated look as we made our way over to the elevator. Ben had undoubtedly caught on to his girlfriend's shenanigans too. I knew Elise had noticed Henri's expression because she wiggled her eyebrows behind him when I turned to her.

I mouthed for her to cut it out. If Elise thought I was going to sleep with another F1 driver, she was out of her mind. I had learned my lesson after Liam.

Formula 1 racing drivers were bad boys, and they were officially off limits.

The group of us arrived at the Silverstone party just after

10 p.m. Once we got there, Henri, Ben, Elise, and I headed straight to the bar, ordering a few more glasses of champagne before we ventured to a table in the corner, idly chatting away about the weekend.

Out of the corner of my eye, I spotted familiar faces – Liam and Charlie had arrived, with Melly trotting shortly behind Charlie, happily chatting away to another woman that I didn't recognize. After a few more moments, I saw the girl lean her head onto Liam's back, giving him a small snuggle as he ordered drinks for the group at the bar. My body went stiff as I watched the two of them. I knew it was ridiculous to feel this wave of jealousy. I couldn't expect him to stay single forever, especially not an F1 driver as attractive as Liam.

I had my chance, and I turned it down – for good reasons, I reminded myself. Dating an F1 driver had never made it onto my dream board as a child. Designing a Championship winning car? Now that had been on my board since I was ten.

Everything within me hoped that Liam and Charlie wouldn't see us sitting in the back corner, but as per usual, the universe had other plans. As soon as Liam and Charlie had their drinks, I could see Charlie make eye contact with Henri, who was waving them over. My body immediately stiffened, which Henri seemed to notice because he put an arm around my shoulders and gave me a squeeze, pulling me closer to him.

"Come on, Poppy, just because they work for Wilmington, doesn't mean you have to ignore them," Henri teased. Everyone in the paddock was aware of my Wilmington job offer – Jack, Wilmington's CEO and Team Principal, was about as subtle as the "b" in the word when it came to making Wilmington's intentions known.

I just awkwardly chuckled and motioned for Henri to scoot over, which he obliged, casually leaving his left arm around my shoulders as we moved, making way for the other two drivers and their dates. Liam immediately saw me and smiled, before letting his smile falter as his eyes moved to Henri's arm around my shoulder. Henri and I were just friends, but I could see why this looked incredibly off to Liam. I'd made a huge deal about not wanting to date a Formula 1 driver, and yet here I was wearing gold, all snuggled up with Henri Dubois at a post-race party.

Even if I hadn't intended for it to look like this, I felt a huge wave of guilt wash over my body.

Liam slid into the booth first, and I jolted my leg away as soon as I felt his touch. It was a small booth, and with an additional four people, it was impossible not to touch him. He flashed me his famous Cheshire cat smile before getting comfortable, letting his leg just slightly ghost mine every so often. Liam and Charlie had purchased a few extra bottles of champagne, and without even asking, Liam was already filling up my glass.

"So, Poppy, you and Ben looked like an absolute firecracker out there," Charlie praised as he cooly sipped his champagne.

"It's all her, mate," Ben laughed, giving me a wink and a high five, which I promptly returned across the table.

"Dream team!"

"Your confidence is inspiring. Although after rejecting that offer Wilmington gave you, I think we're all wondering what dirt Ben has on you." Liam said the words with jest in his tone, but I could sense the underlying meaning – the hint that he felt I had made a mistake. The look on his face told me that he had no problems getting on my last nerves, and quite frankly, he had succeeded.

"I don't know, would you leave a team that had just won

two world championships for a team that hasn't won one in over a decade?"

"Jesus, Pop, go for the jugular," Charlie scoffed. I gave him an apologetic look; sometimes it was easy to forget that he also drove for Wilmington.

I could see Liam's eyes flicker between me and Henri for a moment, before he returned his gaze back to his drink. I knew I should have taken the high road, but in moments like this, it just wasn't as satisfying as the petty one.

"I feel like I've said it before, and I'll say it again, plum just isn't my color. We can't all pull it off like you and Charlie." Charlie waved me off in response, but I knew that was him accepting my apology.

"Well, I'd say gold is your color, mon cherie," Henri whispered, a twinkle in his eye as he gave me a *not-so-subtle* kiss on the cheek. No chance I was going to hide the blush that had crept onto my cheeks. "Feel free to come to Hermes whenever you want to work with a *real* champion."

"Oh, is Luca Rossi hiring a new race engineer?" I teased. Henri rolled his eyes at the sound of his teammate's name and gave my cheeks a light pinch.

After the first round of drinks had been consumed, Liam scooted in closer to me, pouring another round of champagne into my glass.

"I'm good, Liam," I said, choking on the champagne as it went down. "Any more and I'll be tempted to start dancing on top of this table."

"You say that like it's a bad thing," Liam half-whispered, and for a moment, my heart ached at the sight of his smile.

God, I missed that smile so much.

Liam leaned down a little closer as he lightly whispered, "I like the Poppy who makes bad decisions. She somehow always ends up in my bed." Before I could retort something back to Liam, I saw *whatever-her-name-was* lean in to say something to Liam, an annoyed look on her face.

Liam went back to chatting with her, turning his back towards me. I felt a small sense of petty satisfaction at her jealousy as I turned back to Henri, Ben and Elise, rejoining the conversation.

Chapter Four
LIAM

The moment I saw Poppy with Henri at the Silverstone party, my heart felt like it was breaking into a million pieces. We had agreed to just be friends, but I wanted more. My heart sank when I spotted her sitting with Henri, and a wave of jealousy overwhelmed me. Still, I knew that having her as a friend was better than nothing, even if we hadn't actually kept to that agreement, something that was partially my fault. Each time I went to text her something, I just couldn't find it in myself to type out the words.

I missed her laugh, her wickedly funny sense of humor, her body when it was wrapped in my embrace.

I missed everything about her.

I couldn't help but let the self-doubt consume me as I sat and pondered the question that had been gnawing at me since last night: *Why was Henri worthy of her attention and not me?*

In truth, I didn't know if they were actually dating. Henri and Poppy had sat together all night, but Henri hadn't actually made a move on her besides resting his arm around her shoulder, albeit very possessively. I knew Henri was a touchy-feely sort of person, so it was possible they weren't dating – but I couldn't shake the sight of her in that ghastly gold dress.

Fucking Hermes yellow.

My mind was working a million miles a minute, so much so, that I didn't even see Charlie come up to me as he aggressively waved his hand in front of my face.

"Mate, you good there?" Charlie asked as he held out a cup of coffee, motioning for me to take it. I gave him a small nod as I took the cup.

"Wow, you've got it bad," I heard Charlie chuckle to himself. I looked up at him, quirking my eyebrows in question.

"You being deep in thought got anything to do with why Alana didn't come to this weekend's race?"

Alana had been the girl I was *sort of* seeing. It was a casual thing. Melly had introduced us, but apparently after last weekend in Silverstone, Alana had deduced that I still had a thing for Poppy and called our relationship quits.

I'd told her she was wrong, but we both knew I was lying.

"We broke things off."

"Sorry to hear that, Liam." Charlie looked at me expectantly and I knew he was waiting for a reason as to why Alana and I had called it quits, but how could I tell him *'because I'm actually sort of in love with the one woman in the paddock that is frustratingly immune to my charm.'*

"It's fine."

Nice one, Liam, I scolded myself. The look on Charlie's face told me he knew it was anything but fine.

"So... anything between Henri and Poppy? I noticed they were a little snuggly last weekend." At hearing *her* name, I looked up to see who Charlie was speaking to, only to see Ben standing next to my teammate as the three of us waited outside of the FIA conference room. I didn't know if I wanted to slap Charlie or thank him for bringing it up – a little bit of both, if I was being honest. I desperately *wanted* and *didn't want* to know the answer to Charlie's question.

It really depended on the answer.

"Poppy and Henri?" Ben grumbled, a look of disbelief in his eyes. "Henri wishes – not a chance from her, mate. You know Henri, he's a snuggly kind of guy, and they were both drunk, but she ended up coming back to our hotel room and eating pizza until 3 a.m. She and Elise were so drunk, I had to get a late checkout and change our leaving time."

I felt a sudden wave of relief wash over me, which I tried not to show on my face, but judging by Charlie's wiggling eyebrows, I knew he had picked up on my relief. I frantically shook my head behind Ben's back, silently begging Charlie not to say anything.

Charlie was a good friend, but he was the paddock's worst pot stirrer.

"Ah, well, bummer for Henri then," Charlie joked. "You think she's just not into dating drivers?" I gave Charlie a harsh look, silently pleading for him to quit while he was ahead.

"No, she isn't," Ben deadpanned. "And you guys shouldn't be into her either." Ben said the words loudly enough so that the other drivers could hear, and a few of them snickered as they told him to piss off.

I couldn't help but roll my eyes. I knew the asshole hated me after the incident last year, but I didn't think even Ben was cruel enough to sabotage my relationship potential with Poppy. Ben turned and looked at me, and I watched him shift his weight from side to side as he chewed on the inside of his cheek. Clearly, he was remembering the situation with Poppy and I last year.

"Look, she's a private person," was all Ben managed to

add, giving me a quick look. As soon as the conference doors opened, Ben practically sprinted inside.

I grabbed my teammate and slapped him on the shoulder. "Why so curious about Poppy's dating life all of a sudden?" I demanded.

"Why are you sitting here daydreaming of Poppy instead of fighting for the woman you clearly still have a thing for?" Charlie retorted.

"Fucking hate when you answer a question with a question."

But Charlie was right. I hadn't really fought for Poppy last year. At first, I was too scared of losing her as a friend. But as months went by, I realized it was more than that. I didn't want to know why she had suddenly stopped coming to my room at night, why she had stopped watching movies in my bed, why she was turning down my coffee invites.

Because deep down, I knew the truth of why she didn't want me. Why would the successful, incredibly beautiful, and intelligent racing engineer want playboy, model-seducing *"Lead-You-On"* Liam Fitzgerald?

I was a joke. Poppy had a first from Oxford, and I was the F1 driver who was known for not being able to point out all of the countries we raced in on a map. A ridiculous social media challenge that pundits used to laugh at how stupid some of us drivers were.

Ben was right. Poppy could do better – much better.

"Poppy said she just wants to be friends, and I'm going to respect that."

"Did you ask her *why*?" Charlie had a blank look on his face, one that told me he already knew the answer to his question.

Of course, I hadn't asked why.

As if I wanted Poppy to confirm what we both knew was true.

I was too scared of the answer, too scared of the rejection, of being told I wasn't good enough. Last year had been tough with the Wilmington car, and this year was proving just as bad. I didn't need another thing going wrong in my life, so I never asked.

I didn't need Poppy telling me that she didn't think Liam "F1's Biggest Playboy" Fitzgerald wasn't boyfriend material.

"Look, Liam, it's none of my business, but if it were me, I'd be trying to figure out why, and then I would do everything in my power to fix it. I saw you guys last year... you looked like a lot more than *just friends* every time you hung out, that's all I'm saying." Charlie gave me a sad smile and patted my shoulder before finally making his way into the FIA conference room.

As soon as the drivers meeting let out, I made my way to the Wilmington garage, doing my best to avoid the barrage of fans that had started to enter the paddock.

When I passed the Rennen area, I saw her – beautiful brown hair flowing in the wind, hands full of binders and papers – as she walked into the garage. Before I could stop myself, I called out to her.

"Poppy!" My voice startled her, and it must have taken all her concentration to keep those stacks of paper from spilling onto the concrete floor. She stumbled, caught herself, and started again towards the door leading inside the garage, but as soon as she made it to the entrance, she tripped over her untied shoelaces and fell onto the concrete. I ran over to help, pulling her up as I checked her face for cuts.

Poppy quickly bent down to pick up the binders and papers before they blew away. As she regained her posture, she lifted her head and gave me a shy smile and an appreciative nod.

"Thanks, Liam. Wow, that could have been bad." She shoved the binders and various folders into her briefcase.

"Glad you're alright." Poppy gave me another smile and quietly thanked me again as we both stared at each other.

God, why does this feel so awkward?

"You, umm, wanna grab a coffee or you got somewhere to be in a rush?" I asked, motioning to her briefcase stuffed full of papers. Poppy let out a small huff but then unexpectedly nodded her head yes as she smiled up at me. My heart immediately warmed at the sight of her smile.

Fuck, I missed that smile so much.

"Sure, coffee would be great." We walked to the nearest F1 coffee stand and ordered before sitting down at one of the little two-top tables.

"How are you feeling about Toronto?" Poppy asked, finally breaking the awkward air that had surrounded us.

"You know, the brakes still aren't quite right, but the car does feel better this year. I have some hope." I wanted it to not sound quite as sad and pathetic as it came out, but this was *Poppy*. I could never hide my feelings from her, and she knew as much as anyone that the Wilmington car wasn't very good this year.

"If anyone can work it out, it's you." I gave her hand an appreciative squeeze at her praise. Poppy had always been so kind and thoughtful, it's what drew me to her in the first place.

We sat and chatted for another 20 minutes before she announced that she had to leave. I was already 5 minutes late to a Wilmington meeting, but coffee with her had been so lovely I didn't care if I was late.

I didn't want it to end.

When I entered the VIP area of the club, I felt my phone buzz in my pocket.

> Poppy: Good job out there. Told you if anyone could do it, you could. A well-deserved podium.

I smiled at Poppy's text. Forget celebrating my third-place finish, apparently a text from Poppy could set my world on fire.

> Liam: Thanks, P. You here for the party?

> Poppy: Of course! I can't NOT celebrate a Ben race win. Think I'd be fired!

As soon as I looked up from my phone, I heard a familiar voice call my name. "Liam! We're over here!" At the back of the room, I spotted Poppy, Ben, Elise and Henri all sitting together. I bristled at seeing Henri sitting next to Poppy, but reminded myself that they were *just friends* – just like Poppy and I were *just friends*.

At least this time she wasn't wearing a stupid gold dress.

"Congrats Ben!" I called out, taking a seat next to Poppy as I gave her thigh a quick squeeze. "Congrats to you, too." Poppy gave me a warm smile, and I immediately felt my heart squeeze.

"Thanks, Liam. You and Charlie looked good out there. Wilmington seems to be catching up." Ben, surprisingly, shook my hand as I sat down at the table and moved the bottle of champagne over, motioning for me to take a glass and have some. Poppy gave her friend an amused look, and judging by Ben's face, I could tell he was incredibly drunk.

"Yeah, the car is feeling better. Looking forward to Australia in two weeks. I think we might be able to place top ten, maybe even top five."

Noticing that Poppy's drink was empty, I motioned towards the bar. "Wanna grab a drink?"

"Yeah, sure. I'll be right back," she said to Ben, who just nodded in agreement as he snuggled his girlfriend.

Much to my annoyance, Henri also joined us at the bar. As the three of us stood there, waiting for our bartender, I eyed the Hermes driver warily, watching his every move with Poppy as the two chatted about *who-knows-what*. The way he laughed at everything she said made my skin crawl.

"I'm going to head to the bathroom, be right back!" She shoved her drink in my hands as she headed towards the restroom.

Henri and I just stood there for a few moments, both of us awkwardly trying to avoid eye contact with each other, before Henri finally broke the ice. "So, you trying to make a play for Poppy, now?" The gleam in his eyes told me he already knew our history.

Charlie and his fucking big mouth.

"None of your concern, Dubois."

"Just wanted to ask before I take her back to my room and make her see stars all night." The moment he said the taunt, I slammed Poppy's drink down on the counter and took a step into Henri's space.

"Let me get one thing straight. Poppy McIntyre is off limits, to you and every other hungry man in this paddock."

"Oooh, a touchy subject, I see," Henri teased. "If that's the case, then why was she wearing *gold* last weekend?"

"I think the real question you should be asking is why was she wearing *nothing* in my bed." I could tell from the satisfied smirk on Henri's face that he had just won this little exchange. I had promised Poppy to keep that information to myself, but in my jealousy, I couldn't help but taunt the Monagasque driver.

But to my surprise, Henri instead leaned into me, a

serious look replacing his smug one. "If Poppy's what you want Liam, I suggest you start to fight for her. A girl as amazing as her won't be available forever."

Before I could respond, Henri just raised his drink in the air as he made his way back to our table, leaving me dumbfounded at the bar. As soon as Poppy returned, I handed her the drink I had ordered, and I motioned to an empty booth on the other side of the bar, Henri's words still floating around my head.

Henri was right, someone as amazing as Poppy wouldn't be single forever.

"So, how are things with your family?" Poppy sat a little closer to me, and even though I knew it was so she could hear the answer to her question over the loud, thumping music, it felt like a jolt of electricity had shocked me as soon as Poppy touched my shoulder.

"My parents are doing great as is my sister. They're really enjoying life in Australia at the moment. It's hard being away from them and my nephew, so I can't wait to see them next week."

"I'm sure that'll be lovely. It was so nice to meet them last year. They're such lovely people," Poppy hummed, sipping more of her drink.

I nodded in agreement as a nice air settled between us, the awkwardness of earlier today fading away. We'd agreed to be *just friends*, but the more I looked at her, laughing and joking about my family, the less I wanted to be *just friends*.

Hell, in that moment, I wanted to throw her onto the table and make her scream my name over and over again, other people be damned.

But, I didn't.

Instead, we slipped back into our familiar cadence as we discussed what sightseeing she had planned after the Australia Grand Prix. The conversation stayed casual and after another half hour, the rest of the group finally convinced us to join them on the dance floor.

As I watched her dance with Elise, her body swaying to the music, I knew one thing to be true: there was no way I could be *just friends* with Poppy McIntyre.

Chapter Five

POPPY

After that evening in Toronto, it was safe to say that Liam and I had resumed our friendship. By that weekend, we'd quickly fallen back into our familiar candor, our texts now filled with hilarious memes and silly gossip from the paddock. I had missed this part of my friendship with Liam.

Having Liam back in my life felt right – like a hole in my heart was finally being mended.

> Liam: I have a question for you.
>
> Poppy: I have an answer.
>
> Liam: Smart ass.
>
> Liam: You interested in maybe coming to Australia a little early? Do some sightseeing with my family?
>
> Poppy: Idk Liam. I mean the media is going to be all over this Grand Prix.
>
> Liam: What if I got us wigs? I'll even wear a mustache!

Liam: They'd never know it was me. ;-)

I couldn't help but laugh out loud at the thought of us wearing wigs, and part of me knew he wasn't kidding. After a few more texts, Liam finally pulled out the big guns and sent me a photo of his mom's sad face along with a video of her begging me to come.

Poppy: You don't play fair, Liam Fitzgerald.

Liam: All is fair in love and war, Poppy.

Is that what this was? I couldn't speak for Liam's heart, but with every text, it felt like my heart was at war with my brain – and I knew where my brain stood on the matter.

Poppy: Fine, I'll change my flights. Rennen gave me a few days off anyway.

Liam: It's a date!

That's exactly what I was afraid of.

"Earth to Poppy!" I looked up to see Ben smiling at me as he waved his hands in front of my face. "What's got you so distracted, hmm?"

Fuck, I have to tell him.

After that evening in Monaco last year, I finally came clean to Ben, told him how I felt about Liam. He was, unsurprisingly, not pleased with the whole situation, and I knew he was caught off guard by how close Liam and I had gotten, but after a week of us tiptoeing around each other, we had made up. After the second championship win last year, our friendship had never been stronger, and I didn't want to fuck that up.

"So, Ben, I was thinking I might head to Australia early and do a little sightseeing."

"Oh yeah? That could be fun. I'll see if Elis-"

"I'm going with Liam," I blurted out before Ben could finish his sentence, knowing full well he was about to invite him and Elise onto my vacation.

"... Liam? As in Liam Fitzgerald? Fuck, Poppy, I thought you were done with him!"

"We've been chatting a bit recently, and he asked me to come visit. I have time off, so I figured why not."

"Why not? How about because he's a fucking egotistical prick who tried to kill me." I couldn't help but give Ben a look that said: *really?*

"That's a bit of an overstatement," I deadpanned back.

"Really? Were you in the car that flipped several times before catching on fire?"

"Ben..." Before I could reach for his hand, he got up, his face red with frustration and anger.

"It's fine, Poppy. Just let me know when you plan to leave for Wilmington so I can get a *new* racing engineer onboarded." As Ben stormed off, I felt a tear slide down my face as his words hung in the air like a dark cloud ready to rain over a Sunday picnic.

As if on cue, I heard my phone ping and I immediately knew who it was from.

> Elise: Don't worry about him, Poppy. Go to Australia. You deserve the time off!

> Poppy: Ben is quick to tattle tale....

> Poppy: You should have seen the look on his face.

> Elise: I'll deal with his grumpy ass. Go get your man, Poppy.

I arrived in Australia the Saturday before the race weekend, which gave Liam and I a few days to explore Melbourne. Liam took me to all his favorite food spots, a few art museums, and a couple of lovely hikes. I had offered to get my own hotel, but Liam's parents would hear nothing of it.

I was surprised when they offered to put me up in their house that they had rented for the week, but they were both insistent. Sometimes his parents joined us on our expeditions, but more often than not, it was just Liam and I exploring the city together. I was shocked – *and relieved* – at how little paparazzi was around. Felix, my Team Principal and boss, knew I had gone a little early to explore; he had surprisingly even encouraged it, but Rennen didn't particularly want me plastered across Formula 1 gossip sites with Ben's biggest rival.

But just as quickly as it had started, my vacation was over and the grand prix weekend had arrived. After a few disappointing Free Practice sessions, Ben had managed to eke out a half-decent qualifying grid place. I knew our little spat was affecting his performance, and judging by how he tiptoed around me, he knew it too – but for once I decided that it was *his* turn to apologize.

On the Sunday, the Australian paddock was buzzing with Liam Fitzgerald fans. As the only Aussie driver on the circuit, Liam was basically a hero in the paddock. Everywhere I turned I saw his face on a stick somewhere, and he could barely go anywhere without a hoard of fans begging him for signatures.

> Liam: How's it feel to be surrounded by your favorite color?

> Poppy: Wilmington needs a better color. Feel like I am drowning in plum over here.

> Liam: There's worse ways to die. Death by plum actually sounds pretty good to me.
>
> Liam: Btw the parents say hey... we missed you on Friday.

> Poppy: Thanks. Trust me, I would have preferred to be with your family vs. the garage until 2am. I finally had to kick Ben out & make him go get some sleep after that car wreck.

> Liam: If anyone can get that car back together, it's you.

I smiled at Liam's confidence in me, looking at my phone for a moment before contemplating what to send next.

> Poppy: Thanks. You know it'd be easier to do if I wasn't surrounded by Liam Fitzgerald faces everywhere...

I attached a photo of one of the faces I've seen people holding, one with Liam's eyes removed so that the fan could look through the cardboard cut out of his face.

> Liam: I would have thought being surrounded by such a handsome face all day would have made it easier.

> Poppy: One Liam is more than enough.... possibly too much already ;-)

> Liam: How your lies hurt me!
>
> Liam: I know you secretly want more Liam in your life.

If only Liam knew how true that statement was. I typed out a response and then deleted it, only to type out another one, only to delete that.

> Poppy: Well, I can concede to one thing: the world definitely needs more Liam smiles, no doubt about that.
>
> Poppy: Now go shut up and drive, Liam.

Liam: Your wish is my command.

And with that, I put my phone in my bag and made my way to the hotel lobby. I saw Ben standing by his Mercedes as he waved to me. While we hadn't quite made up from the fight we'd had last week before Australia, this morning we had made a peace pact, both of us choosing to ignore the elephant in the room as we focused on what we had come here to do – win a third World Driver's Championship.

Elise was already in the passenger seat. I hopped into the back seat and pulled out my notes so I could start running through some stats with Ben.

"So... how was your week with Liam?" Elise asked. I heard Ben lowly grumble to himself, and I gave Elise a pointed look that asked why on earth she would bring that topic up now, four hours before the start of the Grand Prix.

"Fine. Now Ben-"

"That's all you're going to give us?" Elise cut in. I could see her roll her eyes in the rearview mirror.

"I had a nice time. He's a good *friend*." I put the emphasis on *friend*, hoping Elise would get the point.

Her smile told me she did, but I could tell she was also refusing to acknowledge it.

"I don't understand. Liam is clearly interested. What's stopping you?" Elise turned around to face me, giving me a small smile.

"Now isn't the time for a relationship."

"Especially not with Liam Fitzgerald..." I heard Ben

mutter under his breath. Elise just slapped his arm as she turned back around to face me.

"Oh, come on, age 28 isn't the time for a relationship?"

How exactly was I supposed to tell Elise: '*I don't want to be a driver's girlfriend because the pressure is too much for me.*' Elise was amazing at handling the constant press and paparazzi, and I loved her strong confidence and ability to win over any crowd, but I wasn't her.

I valued my privacy too much, and I was too scared of losing it.

"I am, in fact, happy being single. I don't need a boyfriend to be happy."

"No one said you *needed* one," Elise said a little exasperated. "I'm just confused why you don't *want* one."

"Can we just drop it for now?" I didn't mean for the words to come out of my mouth so harshly, but I was over this conversation.

"Yes, can we?" Ben added. I knew Elise had finally gotten the point as she turned around to face her boyfriend, soothing the side of his face slightly, as she continued to frown at my outburst. After a few more moments of silence, I opened my notebook once again and began reviewing some of the car stats with Ben.

"And there we have it ladies and gentlemen! Liam Fitzgerald finally has his first win of the season!" As I overheard the Sky Sports coverage in the garage, a small smile crept over my face. He'd finally done it.

Liam had managed to win at his home race.

Ben and Charlie had done well, coming in P2 and P3. The crowd rushed to meet the three of them as they parked their cars in their respective podium spots. Ben finally spotted me in the sea of people, and he ran over, giving me a huge hug before giving Elise a big kiss.

"I'm so fucking proud of you, Ben!" I yelled.

"It's all you Poppy. All you!" I smiled at my friend, and I knew I couldn't hide the slight blush on my cheeks. Ben was great at thanking the entire team. He knew getting on the podium was a team effort.

As the podium celebration came to an end, I saw Liam drinking champagne out of his shoe with Charlie, the two of them giggling like little school girls up on the podium. After the podium celebration was done, Elise looped her arms with mine, and we walked back to the Rennen garage.

I took out my phone to send Liam a text, but I noticed that a text was already on the screen from him.

> Liam: Got a glass of champagne in my driver's room waiting for you.
>
> Poppy: Not worried I won't come steal the Wilmington engineering strategy?
>
> Liam: Nothing sexier than a little Formula 1 espionage ;-)

I rolled my eyes at his response, trying to stop a blush from creeping onto my face. Elise didn't need any more ammunition to ask about Liam. I knew I should stay in the Rennen garage, but as I walked back out into the hallway, I heard Felix announce that the team would be able to leave early. We'd worked so hard all weekend, so the debrief would happen back at the offices on Tuesday.

I grabbed my bag and started walking towards the Wilmington hospitality suite. John, Liam's physio and best friend, was waiting outside of the suite, a look of mischief in his eyes. He and I walked back to Liam's room, where he opened the door and snuck us inside. With all the commotion going on around us, no one even noticed me, dressed in red, walk through the Wilmington hospitality suite.

"I'll be right back," I heard John call out. Before I could ask him what was going on, he had already left the room, leaving me to sit alone on the plum-colored couch.

After a few more moments, Liam finally walked into the room, a huge smile on his face. He ran over to me and gave me a huge hug, picking me up in the air and spinning me around. I squealed as he picked me up, wrapping my arms around him.

"So proud of you, Liam!"

He sat me down, and the two of us took a breath as our eyes met. His stare was intense, but his smile was still warm and inviting. I felt pesky butterflies begin to circle, and I suddenly started to feel shy under his gaze.

I shouldn't be feeling this way. We are just friends, I reminded myself.

"So, where is the rest of the Liam Fitzgerald crew? I'm sure everyone wants to celebrate with Wilmington's hero himself?" I teased. Liam ignored my comment, gently placing his hand on my chin, tipping it up as he forced me to look directly into his eyes.

"I love it when you say my name." His words were a tad slurred, and I could tell he was a little tipsy after celebrating on the podium. His eyes kept gazing into mine, and I could see some unspoken words in them – unspoken words and *desire*. The moment felt incredibly intimate, and I knew the blush I was trying to hide had made itself at home on my face. I backed out of his grasp, turning to his table as I grabbed a glass so I could pour myself some champagne.

"So, where are we going to celebrate tonight, then?" My voice was shakier than I would have liked, but Liam just continued to smile as he motioned for me to rejoin him on the couch.

"John has a club booked. I'll text you the details." I nodded in response, downing my glass of champagne. I went to say something, but I heard my phone going off. It was Ben.

"Don't answer it," Liam said, a hint of desperation in his voice. I gave Liam an apologetic look as I answered the phone.

"Hey, Ben!" I could hear a ton of commotion in the background, and I could barely make out what Ben was saying.

"You coming, P? We're about to leave!" I finally heard Ben ask over the roaring crowd.

"Be right there!" I yelled back, and I could see the disappointment grow on Liam's face. "Thanks for the drink, Liam, but I gotta run... Ben drove me today and they're leaving. But I'll see you tonight, yeah?"

I could feel the energy in the room shift. It's as if he was building up to say something but couldn't get the words to come out of his mouth. Still, a sly smile formed on his lips and he nodded at me, taking the glass from my hand.

"Of course. Can't wait!" As I turned to leave, Liam called out to me one more time. "Oh, and Poppy, try and wear something plum tonight, yeah?" He said with a wink.

"You're the worst!" I giggled, checking the Wilmington hallway before making a beeline towards the exit.

As soon as I walked into my hotel room, I kicked off my shoes and jumped onto the bed, collapsing from the exhausting day. The moment my back hit the duvet, I felt something poking me from behind.

Good grief, what is this?

I hopped off the bed and looked down to see what I had landed on. On the bed was a – *now squished* – shopping bag.

The bag was beautiful, with lovely tissue paper coming out of it. Wherever this piece of clothing was from, it was expensive.

"Must be a thank you from Ben... Hopefully an apology for being a dick."

> Poppy: Your apology is accepted.

Ben: For?

> Poppy: Being an ass all weekend.

Ben: Uh huh.

Ben: And how did I apologize for being an ass all weekend?

> Poppy: The gifts left on the bed...

Ben: Is this you asking for a gift? Was the raise I got you this year not enough?

> Poppy: Ha ha, very funny...

I attached a photo of the bag in the text. I could see three dots form on our iMessage thread, then disappear, then form again. As I waited for Ben's response, I went to the bathroom and hopped into the shower, letting the warm water soothe my aching body. Just as my shower finished, I heard my phone ding.

Ben: Poppy, you are family to me. I love you like a sister, and as my sister, I can sincerely say, I would never get you something from that store.

Ben: No offense but... gross.

Ben: But please, let me know who it's from
so I know whose race car to run off the
track next week.

I cocked my eyebrows at his text and then quickly dumped the items out of the bag.

Ahhhh. As the items hit the bed, I immediately understood Ben's comment.

In front of me lay a beautiful lingerie set from Agent Provocateur in bright purple – plum to be more specific. Immediately a text from Elise lit up my phone, and I let out an annoyed sigh. Elise and Ben shared literally everything, and while I loved them both, sometimes I hated their relationship.

Elise: WHO GOT YOU THE LINGERIE?

Elise: AND HOW DO YOU NOT KNOW
THAT BRAND? What, do you live under a
rock?

Poppy: Not all of us can afford 250 pound lingerie.

As a response, I just sent her back a photo of the brightly colored lingerie. Inside the bag was a card, which had fallen out with the bra.

> *"Saw this and thought of you.*
> *Figured you wouldn't have brought something plum with you.*
> *Your Liam xoxo"*

Well, fuck.
I re-read the card no less than ten times. I let my hands

feel the lingerie. It was incredibly soft and beautiful. The price of the set was probably more than all of my bras and underwear put together.

> Elise: So much for being just friends ;-)

So much for being just friends, indeed.

I knew I should be frustrated with Liam. I had made it clear that I was only interested in being friends, but as I put the lingerie set on, I felt my anger start to dissipate. It looked and felt incredible... and I felt sexy wearing it. It was simple yet elegant.

Bastard knew I'd like this set.

After another hour went by, I threw on the dress that I had brought for tonight and made my way downstairs to where I was meeting Elise and Ben, who had resumed his icy personality, no doubt because Elise had let him know who the lingerie was from.

As we hopped into the taxi, Elise leaned over and whispered, "So are you wearing it under your dress?" She wiggled her eyebrows, causing Ben to groan. I was a little horrified that Ben knew I had received the lingerie from Liam, but decided to ignore that nagging part of my brain.

Fuck it, I was wearing 250 pound lingerie, and I looked hot wearing it.

I just gave her a sly smile but said nothing, instead looking down at my phone. The champagne had started to hit, and I was feeling a little bolder.

> Poppy: Wildest thing happened today.

> Liam: Oh?

> Poppy: Someone broke into my room.

Liam: Hope they didn't take anything valuable.

> Poppy: Quite the opposite, my thief left me a gift... so inconvenient of him, my suitcase is already quite full.

Liam: Oh yeah? This thief leave you anything good?

> Poppy: I'd say so, although the color was a little off.

Liam: Well, like I always say, if you don't like the color, nothing is always an option.

Cheeky bastard.

As soon as I read Liam's text we arrived at the Melbourne club. The club promoter shuffled us inside the building and up the stairs to the VIP section that had been rented out for the evening. Charlie immediately spotted us, and he ran over, giving me a hug so tight I could barely breathe as he picked me up and spun me around. Melly was behind him, shaking her head in slight embarrassment. Clearly, the Wilmington team had spent the rest of the evening drinking before coming here.

Elise and Melly each grabbed a hand of mine and dragged me to the bar to order drinks.

"Soooo... you going to give Liam a congratulations present later tonight?" Melly giggled, giving me a knowing look. I looked at Elise, who pretended not to notice my glare, as she ordered from the bartender.

"A polite woman never kiss and tells!"

"Aww, come on Poppy... you're no fun!"

I stuck my tongue out at the two of them as I took my drink from the counter and left, walking back towards the group of guys who had found seats at a booth closer to the back. I sat and chatted to John, Liam's friend, before making my way to the dance floor, grabbing Elise and Melly in the process as I demanded that they dance with me.

As Elise and I swayed to the music, Liam sauntered over and cut in.

"Mind if I have this dance?"

"Liam, surprised you're still standing," I quipped, motioning to the drink in his hand. He had to easily be on his second bottle of champagne.

Liam leaned down, putting his face next to my ear as he whispered, "Don't want to drink too much, princess, or I might not be able to see that little gift the thief left you later tonight." Before I could protest, Liam grabbed my hips, and we continued to dance together, letting the beat of the music set the pace of our swaying.

As the song "6 Inch Heels" came on, I felt Liam step closer to me, letting his hands gently roam up and down my waist as we danced. I wanted to pull away, but the feeling of his hands on me was phenomenal. I had missed Liam's touch – hell, I had missed everything about him. He was incredible in bed and as we danced closer, our bodies tightly wound together, I began to forget all of those reasons why we shouldn't be together.

I knew Liam could tell where my mind was wandering, and he lifted my chin up to face him. "You look so stunning in that dress, Poppy. Absolutely breathtaking."

"What if I told you it's not even the most expensive thing I'm wearing tonight." I could see Liam's face darken, lust filling his green eyes as I turned around, letting my back hit his chest as we continued to dance. I could feel his cock starting to get hard behind me, pushing slightly into my ass as we swayed to the music.

Liam let his lips ghost the shell of my ear as he leaned down, whispering, "Oh really now... sounds like that thief really did leave a nice gift, maybe you should consider thanking them."

"Well, if I'm lucky, he might drop by my room tonight so I can thank him properly."

Liam turned me around to face him once again, his lips still dangerously close to my face as we danced to the music, ignoring everyone around us. It was as if the entire room had disappeared, and it was just Liam and I – not a care in the world.

"True, although now I think about it, Poppy, if a thief has access to your room, maybe it's not safe for you to be there all alone. Perhaps you should stay at a *friends* tonight." I didn't miss the way he emphasized *friends*, a hint of mischief and laugher in his voice.

Prick was mocking me.

"Well, I would, but I think all my friends are a little busy tonight... maybe I should see if Henri is free?" I said nonchalantly, getting some internal satisfaction as I saw Liam clench his jaw at the mention of the Hermes driver.

So he was jealous after seeing Henri and I together. Had Elise... planned that?

Before he could retort something rude about the unlikeliness of that happening, Ben came over and gave Liam a cold handshake, conveniently placing himself between me and the Australian driver.

"Liam, good racing today." Ben's voice told me he was anything but happy for Liam. "Nice of you not to crash me out this time."

"Jesus, Ben..." I grumbled, attempting to make desperate eye contact with Elise, but she and Melly were too engrossed in their conversation to notice.

"There was no point, seeing as how you were *behind me* all race."

Ben stepped closer to Liam, still holding his outstretched

hand. "I understand you coming after me, Liam, but my best friend? Really? Even I thought you were better than using Poppy to hurt me."

"You leave Poppy out of this," Liam demanded. Finally, Elise and Melly had looked up, and I could see Melly frantically calling Charlie over, desperate for him to de-escalate the situation unfolding in front of us.

"Say her name again." I recognized the look in Ben's eyes as he said the words. It was the same look from Brazil two years ago, that look of utter hate and anger.

"Poppppp-" Before Liam could finish his taunt, Ben had managed to get a swing at Liam, but in his drunken state, he had fallen over, and now Liam was on top of Ben, pushing him into the ground. Fortunately, Charlie had seen the interaction, and he was already hauling Liam off of Ben as Henri did the same to Ben, the two of them both frantically pulling towards each other.

Well, I guess they're now even on punches.

Charlie and Henri dragged the two of them into the VIP booth and away from prying eyes.

"Fucking stop!" I yelled as soon as we got into the private area. "What the fuck is wrong with the two of you?"

"He started it!"

"No, he did last year when he tried to kill-"

"Enough!" I yelled, finally getting ahold of their attention.

"Ben, Liam did not try to fucking kill you. That incident was clearly an *accident*." As Liam went to say something, I turned to him, wagging my finger in his face. "An accident that you were at fault for, don't get me wrong, Liam. As much as you want to ignore it, your recklessness was careless. That said, it's been two damn years, Ben. It's time to let it go." Ben just groaned as Elise handed him a coke, the punch from Liam sobering him up with every second that passed.

I turned to Liam as he watched me, and I could see the guilt in his eyes, that same guilt he had shown me two years ago. "Poppy's right, Ben. I was careless, but I mean it when I say I didn't intend to crash you out. I'd never put the safety of a fellow driver over me winning – ever. I hope you can see that."

As Ben let out a deep breath, I could tell that he was contemplating his next words carefully. I motioned for Ben to say something, and after a few more moments, he finally looked over to Liam, who now had a packet of ice wrapped around his hand.

"I just... when you went for Poppy, it felt like you were trying to take away more than my championship, Liam. Like stealing the race win wasn't enough, you also wanted my racing engineer and best friend. I mean why her? Why Poppy?"

"Because I love her." Liam said the words so simply that it took a moment to register what he had said.

Liam loved me?

I turned to look at him, his dark brown hair was drenched in sweat and his eyes were tired, and yet in that moment, I had never found him to be more handsome.

Liam Fitzgerald loved me.

"You really love her?" Ben eyed Liam cautiously, a look of shock on his face as if he couldn't possibly comprehend what Liam was saying.

"I love the way she weighs her coffee every morning, down the the ounce, so that she can get the perfect cup of coffee. I love that she laughs at the most awkward movie scenes at the most inappropriate times. I love how when she steps out into snow, she always immediately does a snow angel, no matter the place." Liam took a deep breath in, before finally exhaling. "My heart burns for her, Ben. She's the first person I think of in the morning, and the last person I dream of at night."

Finally, he turned to me. "Poppy, I'm sor-"

"Did you just say you love me?" I interrupted him, not wanting to let his little speech drag on any longer than it had to.

"I did... I do."

I slowly walked towards Liam, pushing him back into the sofa as I straddled his lap.

"Poppy, you don't have to-"

"Shut up and kiss me, Liam Fitzgerald." Liam didn't have to be told twice. The way he kissed me made me forget about the fact that we were in a closed off area of the club, made me forget that there were several other drivers around us, until a whistling sound caught me off guard, bringing me back into reality.

"You guys gonna get a room or what?" Charlie chuckled. I turned back around to face my friends, my face red with embarrassment as I realized that I was still straddling Liam, my dress now slightly hiked up my legs.

"Alright... alright." I looked over to Ben, and he gave me a small, but genuine, smile. "I-I didn't realize you loved her." Ben walked over to me and gave me a hug and kiss on the cheek, before ruffling my hair, before giving Liam a determined glare. "I meant what I said in Monaco, Liam. You hurt Poppy, and I'll be the one running your car off the track, are we clear?"

"Crystal." Liam finally set the ice down onto the table as he took Ben's outstretched hand and shook it. For the first time in two years, they finally exchanged a *genuine* handshake.

"Well, well, hell must have frozen over," Elise chuckled as she poked Ben in his side. His look told her that he wasn't quite ready to joke about it, but the softness of his face told me that while he wasn't thrilled about this development, he was okay with it.

And that was all I needed.

I looked at the clock, realizing that it had reached almost midnight, and after the events of tonight, I was exhausted. I turned to Liam, not quite sure of what to say, but he just smiled at me, that mischievous Cheshire cat grin.

"So... if I remember correctly, someone needed a place to sleep tonight, no?"

"That's the rumor, Fitzgerald. You know of a place?"

With minutes Liam had shuffled us into the back of a taxi. As soon as Liam told the driver the hotel address, his lips were on mine. The kiss was hot and passionate, full of lust. Our tongues were both fighting for dominance over the other as Liam wrapped his hands around my waist and pulled me as close to him as possible. Fortunately, the club was a very short distance from the Wilmington hotel. Liam pulled me out of the cab and made quick work of getting us into the elevator. As we stepped inside, I saw a group of VIPs standing there, chatting away. They gave Liam some compliments on the race, before the elevator door rang for Liam's floor. He dragged me to his hotel room and quickly opened the door.

Before I could say anything, he picked me up and threw me on top of the bed, licking his lips as he looked down at me.

"Before this continues, Poppy... I have to ask, are you sure you want to do this?" Liam moved closer to me, his pupils now completely blown with lust and desire. He leaned over me and gazed intently into my eyes; the question lingered in the air for just a little while longer.

"Yes," I finally breathed out in a whisper.

"Good, because after tonight, I don't think we can go back to being friends."

"Fuck it, we were pretty terrible at being friends anyway," I grinned, earning a chuckle from Liam as he tore my dress over my shoulders, leaving me in my heals and plum lingerie set.

Liam crawled over me and kissed my lips, before trailing his sloppy kisses down my neck and chest, making sure to pay attention to every mole and mark that he saw. I whined a bit as Liam paid close attention to each of my breasts, giving them the attention he said they deserved. After a few more moments, he began to make his way down my body to where I wanted him most. He slowly pulled my beautiful lacy underwear off, throwing it to the back of the room. I sighed at the contact when his lips left soft kisses around my core, opening my legs a little bit more and pushing myself down. I heard a snicker come from Liam, and I gave him a little pout as he looked up at me, a devious grin and twinkle in his eyes.

"You're so fucking beautiful. I love everything about your body, all the way down to each of your moles."

I felt myself blush, not that Liam could see it, as he dove into my core like a man starved. Liam's tongue began to work its way around my clit, never getting quite as close as I wanted him to as he continued to tease and taste me.

It didn't take Liam long to get me to my first orgasm. As soon as it hit me, I began chanting his name, grabbing the sheets with both my hands as the bliss tore through my body. When I opened my eyes, the first thing I saw was Liam looking up at me with his beautiful green eyes, saliva running down his chin as he licked his lips, clearly enjoying the taste of my juices.

That should not have turned me on as much as it did.

As Liam began to crawl up my body, I stopped him and

took the opportunity to switch us, causing Liam to fall onto his back as I sat on top of his thighs.

"Fuck Liam, I don't know what it is about this chest tattoo, but it's so damn hot." Liam just smirked at my reaction, grabbing my hips with both of his large hands to steady me as I observed his tattoo.

"You want to ride me, baby girl?"

I nodded eagerly, lifting my hips as he situated himself underneath me. I began to let myself sink onto him, gasping as he began to fill me up. I had forgotten how big he was, and even though he had prepped my body, he still felt massive. I let myself revel in the feeling of him for a moment, slowly moving my hips back and forth to get some friction on my clit. As if on cue, Liam brought his hand to where I wanted him most and began to rub slow circles.

At first, the overstimulation made me stop, but as Liam kept going at a savagely slow pace, I began to feel myself hurdling toward that pleasure I remembered all too well.

"Oh, fuck, Liam – don't stop." I continued to bounce up and down, letting my hands steady myself on his chest for extra balance as I could feel myself beginning to reach my second orgasm of the night. Liam let out a string of grunts and groans, and I could tell that he was getting closer.

"Come with me, baby girl," he begged – *well, pleaded* – as he began thrusting up into me as I came down on him, his hand working furiously as he tried to bring me closer to my high.

After a few more moments, I felt my walls begin to flutter around his length. I fell forward as I reached my climax. Liam thrusted a few more times before letting out a guttural sound, calling out my name as I began to feel his cum drip down my legs.

We both lay there on the bed, attempting to catch our breaths. Finally, Liam moved me off of him and laid me down as he got up from the bed and headed to the bathroom. He returned with a warm washcloth and cleaned me up, before throwing it on the floor and grabbing a bottle of water from the fridge.

"That was..." he began, not being able to find the words.

"Yeah..."

"Glad you liked the lingerie."

"Bold move dropping off lingerie at my hotel room." Liam rejoined me on the bed and pulled me closer in to him, draping my spent body over his.

"I meant what I wrote in the note. I saw the set and immediately thought of you. Well, I immediately thought of me pulling it off of you," he winked.

I slapped his chest playfully, taking another moment to admire his tattoo, and we fell back into a comfortable silence. I knew I had to ask the question that was hanging over us, a question I knew we both wanted to avoid. Finally, Liam flipped me onto my back, his body now hovering over me. His face was only inches from mine and he gave my lips a gentle peck. I felt his hands rub up and down my waist in soothing motions.

"Why did you want to be *just friends* last year?" His words were gentle as he brought one hand up to caress my face, moving some hair out of my eyes in the process.

"I don't know, Liam," I began, but he stopped me with another peck on my lips.

"I can tell you why I didn't fight for you." His words took me by surprise, and I paused, looking deeply into his eyes, curious about what he was going to say. "I didn't fight because I was scared you would reject me. Scared you would get tired of me and my jokes. Scared you would be embarrassed about how I was driving the car, about how poorly I was doing in the championship." He said the last part so low, I barely heard him.

I raised my head and pecked his lips, letting a small smile cross my face. "You were worried I'd be embarrassed to be seen with you?" I asked, confusion laced in my voice. Liam just nodded in response.

I felt a pit in my stomach. I had denied Liam because of my own insecurities, but as listened to how he felt, I felt silly – stupid even. I felt terrible that I had made him feel that way by denying our relationship, never giving him a reason why.

But I knew why I didn't tell him the reason – because he would have told me I was being ridiculous. That no matter what the journalists, gossip blogs or fans said, he'd always find me to be beautiful. He would have convinced me it was all okay, tearing down the walls I had built up in the process.

I didn't tell him the reason because I was scared, but as I looked into his eyes, all of those fears began to dissipate.

"I said I wanted to be friends, Liam, because *I* was scared. Scared of being an F1 driver's girlfriend. Scared that people would think I wasn't worthy enough to be your girlfriend, or that sleeping with you might get me promotions I wouldn't otherwise get. Scared of losing my privacy…"

I hated how small my voice was when the words came out of my mouth, but as I looked up at Liam, I saw a huge grin on his face. "You, F1's most savage engineer and 2x title holder, were scared you weren't worthy enough?" Liam let out a laugh of disbelief.

"Babe, fuck anyone who doesn't think you're worthy enough. Any promotions you get are backed up by phenomenal results from you and Ben. You're incredibly intelligent and beautiful." Liam leaned down to give me another kiss on the lips.

"So where does this leave us?"

"There hasn't been a day where I haven't thought about you," Liam admitted. "I still want to take you out, show you off to the world, tell everyone that I have this amazing girlfriend. But I totally understand your need for privacy. So, I'd like to take this slow, do things the right way."

"Yeah?"

Liam nodded, letting his body rest next to me. I turned to face him and gave his cheek a kiss as I snuggled in closer. "You drive a hard bargain, Fitzgerald. Quite the negotiator."

"Oh yeah? Well, maybe there is still hope of me convincing you to become my engineer after all." Before I could protest, I felt his lips on mine again.

"I love you, Liam Fitzgerald." I could see the emotion in Liam's eyes as I told him those three little words I had wanted to say all season.

"Poppy McIntyre, you don't even know the meaning of the word, but by tomorrow morning, you *definitely* will."

Liam kept to his promise, making sure to show me exactly how much he loved me.

EPILOGUE

Poppy

"Hey, Elise!" I looked down at my phone, hoping that Elise couldn't hear my hands shaking.

"What's up, Pop? It's a little early-"

"Guess who you're talking to?" I couldn't help but let out a squeal of excitement.

"Poppy, its 7 a.m. in the morning on a Saturday, I cannot for the life of m-"

"You're talking to Valkyrie F1's newest Engineering Director."

"Shut! The! Fuck! Up!" I could hear Elise screaming on the other end of the line, which was met by an equally loud groan from Ben. I'd told Ben yesterday that I had received the offer, and while I knew my friend was disappointed that I was leaving the team, he had also been incredibly supportive of my decision.

Valkyrie was starting an all-new Formula 1 team, run by women with two female drivers, the first of its kind. When Isabelle, the Team Principal, had approached me with the offer, it was too good to turn down.

"Yes ma'am. I will officially be on their car design team."

"Fuck, Poppy. That's incredible. You were looking for a new adventure... and now you've found one."

"I'm feeling good about this one, Elise. I think this team could be the start of something big, especially for women in motorsport."

"Well, if anyone's going to help the first female Formula 1 driver in four decades win the championship, we know it's you, Pop."

I thanked my friend and quickly hung up the phone, before turning back to my sleeping boyfriend, who was now groggily rubbing his eyes. Liam was still upset I still hadn't taken the Wilmington offer, but even he had to admit, this opportunity was too good to pass up.

I wanted to make a statement in the F1 world, wanted everyone to know that women could be more than grid girls – we could be engineers, Team Principals and drivers. With this opportunity from Valkyrie, I finally had that chance.

INTERESTED IN LEARNING MORE ABOUT THE VALKYRIE F1 TEAM? CHECK OUT GRACE'S DEBUT NOVEL "A MAN'S WORLD" - OUT NOW!

She's a fearless racer with a point to prove. He's her #1 enemy on the grid. Now their careers depend on convincing the world of their love, but can they put aside their past to save their future?

A Man's World is available on Amazon Kindle Unlimited, e-Book and paperback.

Georgia has shattered the glass ceiling of Formula 1 as the newest female racer to join the Valkyrie F1 racing team, an innovative, all-female-run outfit with a mission to smash gender barriers in motorsport. Her lifelong dream of competing alongside her twin brother, Henri Dubois, has finally become a reality. Her singular focus? To claim the title of World Driver's Champion, a feat no woman has achieved before. However, when Georgia's career is imperiled by the media's unfair portrayal and skeptical sponsors, her team hatches an audacious plan to change public perception. Their solution: Georgia should date the charming but egotistical playboy of F1, Luca Rossi.

Luca's life has been a whirlwind of charisma and charm, until an infamous yacht incident in Majorca tarnishes his image, branding him as a reckless playboy. Facing the threat of losing his prestigious Hermes F1 driver's seat, Luca is presented with an ultimatum - mend his reputation or face the consequences. The catch? The person chosen to reform his image is none other than Georgia Dubois, his #1 nemesis on the F1 grid and teammate's most cherished sister. She is sharp-tongued and insufferable, and Luca knows she still harbors resentment for how he treated her all those years ago.

Follow me on social media for more updates & stories!

Instagram | TikTok

ABOUT THE AUTHOR

Meet debut author Grace Newman, a passionate romance author who loves nothing more than a spicy romance novel and a good espresso martini. With Grace Newman, readers can expect sassy heroines who shatter glass ceilings in their battles for gender equality and captivating love stories that blur the lines of love and rivalry.

When Grace isn't immersed in the world of romance, you'll often find her on the racquetball court, where her competitive spirit forgets about her lack of hand-eye coordination, or training whatever newest foster dog has captured her heart. Grace's life is enriched by her two great loves: her devoted husband, who shares her passion for adventure and her love for all things fast (especially Formula 1), and her hilarious dog Daisy, her most loyal companion who listens intently to every plot twist and provides endless inspiration with her wagging tail. Whether they're exploring California's beautiful National Parks or sharing quiet moments at home, these two are Grace's biggest supporters.

Printed in Great Britain
by Amazon